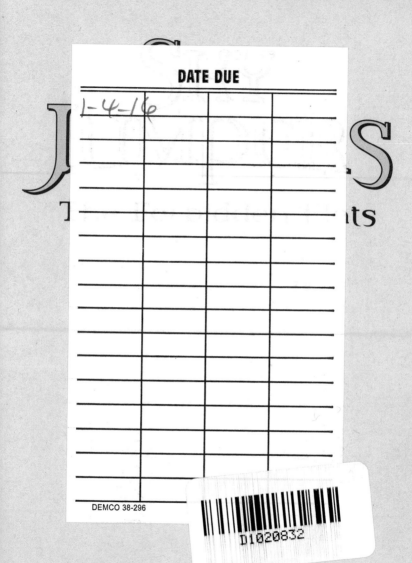

ALSO BY PEGGY EDDLEMAN

*Sky Jumpers*

# SKY JUMPERS

## Book 2
## The Forbidden Flats

### PEGGY EDDLEMAN

A Yearling Book

This is a work of fiction. Names, characters, places, and incidents either are the product of the author's imagination or are used fictitiously. Any resemblance to actual persons, living or dead, events, or locales is entirely coincidental.

Text copyright © 2014 by Peggy Eddleman
Cover art copyright © 2014 by Owen Richardson

All rights reserved. Published in the United States by Yearling, an imprint of Random House Children's Books, a division of Penguin Random House LLC, New York. Originally published in hardcover in the United States by Random House Children's Books, New York, in 2014.

Yearling and the jumping horse design are registered trademarks of Penguin Random House LLC.

Visit us on the Web! randomhousekids.com

Educators and librarians, for a variety of teaching tools, visit us at RHTeachersLibrarians.com

The Library of Congress has cataloged the hardcover edition of this work as follows:
Eddleman, Peggy, author.
The Forbidden Flats / Peggy Eddleman.
p. cm. — (Sky jumpers ; Book 2)
Summary: When an earthquake causes the deadly band of air that covers the post–World War III Earth to begin to sink over the town of White Rock, twelve-year-old Hope must lead a team through the Bomb's Breath and across the Forbidden Flats to obtain the mineral which will save the town.
ISBN 978-0-307-98131-8 (trade) — ISBN 978-0-307-98132-5 (lib. bdg.) — ISBN 978-0-307-98133-2 (ebook)
[1. Survival—Juvenile fiction. 2. Dystopias—Juvenile fiction. 3. Quests (Expeditions)—Juvenile fiction. 4. Adventure stories. [1. Science fiction. 2. Survival—Fiction. 3. Adventure and adventurers—Fiction.] I. Title.
PZ7.E2129Fo 2014  813.6—dc23  2013035051

ISBN 978-0-307-98134-9 (pbk.)

Printed in the United States of America

10 9 8 7 6 5 4 3 2 1

First Yearling Edition 2015

Random House Children's Books supports
the First Amendment and celebrates the right to read.

*To Kyle, Cory, and Alecia*
*Your support is incredible, your laughing is*
*contagious, your love is everything.*

# SKY JUMPERS

## The Forbidden Flats

# The Search

I found a foothold on the rough bark of a tree trunk and climbed up in search of Ameiphus. The plants were a lot harder to spot now, since the freezing winter temperatures turned the normally round green leaves as brown and crinkled as the bark they grew on. I swung my leg onto a branch where one was rooted right next to the trunk. The most important part—the whitish mold in the center where all the leaves came together—was still visible. I pulled a flat rock out of my pocket to dig the Ameiphus loose.

Sitting on a branch this high up, on the outside of the mountain crater my town lived in, gave me the best view of the Forbidden Flats. They stretched on as far as I could see. Unlike the last time I saw them—when the bandits attacked four months ago—they were no longer covered in snow. Now they were covered in mud, with tiny grasses and weeds shooting up everywhere. Mr. Allen, my history teacher, said that before the green bombs of World War III, most of this area was farmland that helped to feed an entire nation of people. The weeds and grasses kind of looked like crops—I wondered if springtime back then looked much different.

"Hope!" Brock yelled from the tree next to me as he pushed the dark hair off his forehead. "Staring at the scenery isn't part of our plan!"

I shook myself out of my surroundings-induced stupor and held out the Ameiphus to where it wouldn't hit any branches. Then I dropped it into the bag Aaren clutched down below.

"Got it!" Aaren called. "We're at seventeen!" I could see his grin even from my height.

I spied another Ameiphus plant a little higher, so I climbed up to it. White Rock's council had decided we should find more Ameiphus and process it into the medicine that cured Shadel's Sickness, because people outside our town needed it as much as we did. Not only would it make a valuable trade product, but White Rock would be less of a target if everyone wasn't so desperate for it.

The small forest inside White Rock barely provided enough Ameiphus for our town. But the area outside of our ten-mile-wide crater was covered in forests, too. Dr. Grenwood figured that at least half would get the ideal amount of sunlight for Ameiphus to grow. The best time to harvest was in fall, but she found a way to salvage a lot of the Ameiphus that had been frozen over the winter.

Crews had been coming out here for weeks, gathering what they could. Brock, Aaren, and I went to the council to convince them that we were old enough to leave the protection of our valley and help search. Of course they said no when *I* asked, but luckily for us, adults loved Aaren and he could talk them into anything. Today they let us join the six others who searched the forest floors as we climbed the trees. Our plan was to gather so much Ameiphus that they'd want to send us out here all the time.

Which meant I needed to climb more than gawk. I found a clump of Ameiphus in the crook where almost every branch met the trunk. I dropped it into Aaren's bag and climbed higher. Before long, I was up so high that Aaren looked like a little squirrel, running around to catch the Ameiphus as Brock and I let go of each one.

"I'm going to get more than you!" I shouted to Brock.

"Not a chance," he said, dropping another clump into Aaren's bag.

A bird landed on the branch next to me and cocked his head to the side. I glanced up. I was at least forty feet high already, but the tree went on for a dozen more. I didn't have to worry about climbing high enough that my head would be in the Bomb's Breath, the fifteen-foot-thick band of invisible but deadly air that covered our valley and everywhere else in the world. None of the other people with us were willing to go high enough up the mountain to be anywhere near it, especially since there weren't any warning fences outside our crater. But I wasn't sure if any of the higher branches would hold me.

"I got another." Brock wasn't in sight, but I could hear the smirk in his voice.

Whatever. I could find more than him if I could get down more quickly than I got up. I swung from my branch to get to the one below me.

"Careful!" Aaren's warning reached me right when I realized that my feet couldn't touch the branch below me.

I made the mistake of looking down to see how far I was from the next branch, but I couldn't see it—I only saw my feet, flailing high above the ground. For the first time ever, the height made me dizzy. I held on tightly with one hand and inched the other along the branch toward the trunk. A few of the people who searched close to us must have seen me, because I heard their shouts of concern along with Aaren's and Brock's. I kept reaching out with my foot, trying to catch the trunk, but every time I missed, I swung back and forth and had a harder time holding on. Then everything went quiet. Brock, Aaren, the others— even the birds seemed to hold their breath. I hooked my foot around the trunk, then pulled myself close enough to hug it with my legs. Relief exhaled out of me.

"You okay?" Aaren shouted.

"I think so." I shifted my shaking hands along the branch toward the trunk with more caution than I'd used since we left White Rock two hours earlier. My arms trembled so much, it felt like the entire tree was shaking.

I heard screams from Brock in a tree to my right, along with screams from everyone on the ground. Then I noticed it wasn't actually me that was shaking—it was the tree! The branches swayed as if in a gale-force wind, yet there was no wind at all.

"Hope!" Aaren's terrified voice me made me freeze. I peered down in horror to see what could make my tree move so violently, when I noticed it wasn't only my tree. It was *everything*.

Before long, Brock joined Aaren on the ground, and they both looked as if they couldn't decide whether to run for their lives or stay to save me. I made myself look away from them and focus on moving my hands along until I got to where I could grab hold of the tree trunk. A terrible rumbling echoed off the mountainside, and all our attention jerked to an area one hundred feet to the west, where the earth ripped open as easily as tearing paper. And the crack was traveling in my direction!

I scrambled down the trunk as quickly as I could manage. I grabbed the branches, not even caring that they were ripping up my hands. Getting to the ground fast was all that mattered. My foot slipped and I slid, my cheek scraping the trunk, until I hit a branch.

"You're halfway here!" Aaren yelled. "You can make it!"

I stretched my foot to another branch farther below. Twenty feet more, and I'd be on the ground. Just twenty feet. A loud *crack* sounded all around me and my tree gave a sudden lurch, then swayed, and I knew the split in the ground had reached its roots. The roaring was so loud, I could barely hear anything else. I stayed hugging the trunk with one arm and caught hold of a branch above my head with the other as it began to topple.

Trees cracked and branches broke and people screamed and my heart beat in my ears like the booms that sounded through the depths of the mountain as the tree fell closer and closer to the ground. I tightened my grip and squeezed my eyes shut, but my stomach still knew I was dropping fast.

The tree stopped so suddenly in midair that my legs lost their grip on the trunk and my hands were nearly ripped off the branch. I opened my eyes to see that the trunk had landed against another massive tree that still stood, keeping mine from falling all the way to the ground.

Below me, Brock and Aaren yelled, "Hope, jump!"

I couldn't. A voice inside me screamed *Hang on!* All I could do was clutch the tree with every bit of strength I had.

"Jump! We'll catch you!" I wasn't sure who said it— Brock and Aaren both stood five feet below my legs with their arms outstretched.

*Get out of here!* a voice inside me pleaded, but I couldn't. Then the *Get out of here!* voice shouted louder than the *Hang on!* voice. I let go and fell.

My body slammed into Aaren and Brock, and we all crashed to the ground. My head was so full of the sounds of the tearing, shaking earth and the need to run that I couldn't tell which body parts hurt. Aaren, Brock, and I struggled to our feet. The ground jerked violently, and I could barely stay upright. We ran, tripped, fell, picked ourselves up, and ran some more, stumble after stumble. Away from the trees crashing to the ground. Away from the earth tearing into pieces. Away from the shaking. Just away.

The earth lurched and we all fell. I tumble-rolled over Brock and down a steep slope, and Aaren landed on top of me at the bottom. I got to my feet, but my legs wouldn't hold me for long before the shaking knocked me back to the ground. Aaren and Brock stood up, their arms out and knees bent and wobbling. We grabbed each other's hands, fearing that one of us would fall away if we let go, and we kept running.

I noticed that two of the six people who were searching for Ameiphus with us were staggering down a hill to the side. I had no idea where the other four were. My lungs burned, but we kept running, trying to escape the crashing trees and splitting earth.

As suddenly as it started, the shaking stopped. Aaren, Brock, and I dropped to the ground, gasping for air. I lay on the forest floor, clutching at weeds, grasses, rocks, and sticks as if they could hold me in place. It felt like the earthquake still shook inside me. I pulled my necklace from under my shirt, held the rough stone pendant from my birth parents, and stroked my thumb and finger down the smooth silver chain from my adoptive parents. Over and over again I rubbed the necklace, as though everything bad would stop if I did.

Before any of us caught our breath enough to speak, I heard shouts in the distance. The other four. Mr. Williams and Stott hobbled toward us with Ben Davies between them, his shirt torn, his arms over their shoulders. Helen Johnson held her arm, which must have been injured. They limped their way to us and collapsed on the ground.

"What was that?" I choked through the dust that coated my throat.

"Earthquake," Stott said.

I shook my head. "An earthquake can't be that bad, can it?"

"They can be that bad." Mr. Williams looked at the mountain where it curved out of sight, toward home. "We need to get back into White Rock. See the damage." He turned to the base of the mountain. "The horses are gone. We'll have to walk."

# A Crack in the Earth

All nine of us stumbled our way around the crater with trembling legs and frazzled nerves for two hours and three aftershocks, until we finally reached the tunnel into White Rock. None of us talked. I think we were all afraid of what we might see. I grasped my necklace almost the whole way and told myself I'd find my parents soon.

At the opening to the tunnel that led us and the river into town, we froze. I looked up at the ceiling of the cave, and thought of the miles of rock that lay above it. Miles of rock that could come crashing down on us if another aftershock hit.

We waited there for an eternity, not moving, before

Mr. Williams said, "Well, we can't stand out here all day." He adjusted Ben Davies's arm over his shoulder, and he, Ben, and Stott took a shuffling step into the tunnel.

I clutched Aaren's hand with my right and Brock's hand with my left, then followed Mr. Williams. It was a million times worse than being in the tree. The seams of white rock cutting across the mostly black ceiling a dozen feet above me had never looked dangerous before, but now it seemed as if chunks bigger than my house were waiting to fall on us. Dust covered the floor of the tunnel, like it had shaken down from the ceiling above, and the river carried broken tree branches and tumbling rocks.

This main tunnel was wide and tall and the few times I had been through it, I'd always felt safe. It wasn't at all like the tunnel on the other side of the crater, where White Rock River exited our valley, that we had crawled through months ago when bandits attacked. Yet right now, this tunnel felt even scarier than that one. I made myself look at the sunlight coming from the other end of the tunnel, a half mile ahead of us.

Every few minutes we'd hear a deep groan coming from inside the mountain itself, followed by rock dust raining down on us. For the first two groans, I managed to keep my eyes on the river. For the third groan, though, I looked up. The thought of it all falling on us made me take off running, Brock and Aaren at my sides, to the end of the tunnel.

"Whoa," Aaren whispered as we burst out into sunlight again.

We stood on the third ring—at one of the best vantage points into our valley. Each flat ring leading up and out from City Circle was a half mile wide, like a step that went in a complete circle. A packed gravel road ran along the back of each ring right before the hill leading up to the next ring, and every single one was damaged. Sometimes broken in large chunks, sometimes with cracks, and sometimes with uneven rises or drop-offs. White Rock River flowed along the third ring toward the south side of the valley, where it spilled into a small lake before exiting through the mountain. The shaking had made the river overflow, and the water streamed all the way down to the runoff ditches around City Circle.

Houses and farms were broken up all around the first three rings, but the worst ones were straight across the valley from where we stood. A couple looked as though they were cracked in half. The roofs of several buildings had buckled in on themselves, or their walls had fallen to the ground. Many of the poles for the grain trams had fallen, and two steam trains had toppled over on their sides. Quite a few barns and sheds had completely collapsed.

My parents might've been home when the first earthquake hit, but I couldn't see our house from here, so I didn't know how badly it had been damaged. My dad could've been working at his split job in the lumber mill. I squinted at the mill a half mile to my left. It looked okay—from the outside, at least.

"Over there," I said. Aaren and Brock looked the same direction I did—to the north, where the warning fences had fallen from the earthquake, and two cows that had probably gotten spooked had gone through the broken fence and charged up the hillside right into the air of the Bomb's Breath. They lay dead at the base of it.

Helen gasped as she stepped out of the tunnel and let out a sobbing hiccup.

"The woods," Brock whispered.

My eyes had been so focused on where my parents might be, I had missed the most obvious problem. It looked as if a giant monster had left claw marks in the side of the mountain, ripping open massive crevices in the clearing at the edge of the woods.

Mr. Williams, Stott, and Ben Davies came up behind me. Mr. Williams glanced at the mines, where he worked at his split, and I noticed for the first time that the main one was caved in, the entrance completely closed. But I could tell he wasn't thinking of his split job of running the mines as much as his job as council member. He'd been voted to take my dad's spot when my dad became the council head. "Come on," he said. "They'll need help."

The posts for the grain tram closest to us were mostly upright, and the rope that stretched from the top of the posts all the way to City Circle looked tight enough to hold the tram platform that hung from the line. Since it was the quickest way down, the ones most injured in our group situated themselves on the platform first; then gravity carried them along the pathway to the community center for help.

Once they reached the bottom, we pulled the cables to bring the tram back up; then the five of us who remained climbed onto the suspended platform. Mr. Williams sat at the brakes and took us down slowly enough to get a good look at all the damage we passed. Everything was worse the closer we got to City Circle.

When we neared the end of the line, Aaren, Brock, and I hopped off the tram and raced across City Circle Road to the small courtyard by the community center, where we had school. It was our town's designated report-in area in case of emergency, and the one place I knew my parents would be if they could make it.

Tons of injured people filled the courtyard. My dad leaned up against the building, clipboard in hand. I could tell that the leg in which he'd been shot months ago was bothering him more than normal by the way he stood.

"Dad!" I yelled, running to him.

Relief washed over his face as he limped toward me and lifted me off the ground in a tight hug. "Are you okay?" He pulled back to make sure nothing was broken and looked at my scraped-up hands and bruised arms.

I brushed the hair out of my face. "I'm fine. What about Mom?"

"She's fine, too. She went inside to get more bandages."

I glanced at all the people in the courtyard. "How bad is it?"

"It's bad. Half the town hasn't reported in yet, and Dr. Grenwood's already got more injured than she can help."

Aaren took off running before my dad finished his sentence. Besides his mom, Aaren knew more about being a doctor than anyone else in White Rock. I hadn't even turned toward the building when two horses raced into the courtyard, carrying Aaren's brother Travin, Mr. Williams's son Pax, and my cousin Carina. My breath left my lungs when I saw her pained face.

"My leg," Carina whimpered as Pax lowered her to Travin. He rushed her toward the several dozen people in the courtyard, Brock and me following closely behind.

Some of the injured were already in casts, some were

walking around, and some were lying in makeshift beds. Most were still waiting their turn. I sprinted ahead of Travin and Carina as my mom came out of the building with her arms full of new bandages.

"Hope!" She set everything down and wrapped her arms around me. "Are you hurt?"

I shook my head. "Why is everyone out here?"

"Too much broken glass inside," my mom said. She picked up the bandages and we headed over to where Mr. Williams's wife was wrapping cuts on people not injured as badly as the ones Dr. Grenwood was treating.

"Where should we help?" I asked.

"It looks like Aaren and his mom are setting Carina's broken leg. She'll have to move on to the next person as quickly as she can, so help Aaren put a cast on it. I think Carina will be glad you're there."

We had only taken three paces toward them when the ground began to shake again. I screamed, adding my voice to the din of all the others as I hit the ground.

"Stay calm!" Dr. Grenwood called over the noise. "It's only an aftershock! Everything will be fine!"

It felt anything but fine. I closed my eyes for a moment to block everything out, but then I couldn't tell which direction was up. My eyes flew back open in time to see the outside window of the Fours & Fives classroom, which the previous quakes had somehow missed, crash to the ground, shattering into pieces, causing a new round of frightened screams.

When the tremors finally stopped, I was crouching on the ground, my shaking arms wrapped around my legs.

"It's over!" Aaren's mom yelled. "If you're not too hurt to help, find something to do. An aftershock that strong is sure to bring more injured. *Move!*"

I forced myself to get to my feet and scrambled toward Carina.

# Sky Jumping

Four days after the quakes, Brock, Aaren, Jella Johnson, and I took hold of a wall frame on the ground next to the Johnsons' house and pushed it upright, replacing their missing wall. Jella's dad, mom, and older brothers nailed it into place. Aaren's little sister Brenna dug in the dirt not far from where we worked. Cleanup began the day after the quakes, and it had taken us this long to remove all the damaged parts of the Johnsons' house so we could start rebuilding it today. We were so exhausted from the work, we slumped against one of the house's good walls while they hammered.

Jella's dad squinted up at the afternoon sun and then at us. "You've all been working hard. Tell you what—we'll finish up this wall. You kids take a break for an hour or two."

Brock pumped his fist. "Yes!"

"What should we do?" Aaren asked.

I motioned in the general direction of the cliffs where we usually sky jumped into the Bomb's Breath. "I think I want to go hiking." The entire town knew that we had gone through the Bomb's Breath when the bandits were here, but it was still deadly, and no one thought we should ever go through it again. With Jella's family close enough to hear, I wasn't about to mention it.

Brock grinned. "I could definitely use a hike."

"Really?" Jella said. "I was thinking of taking a nap."

"As nice as that sounds," Aaren said, "I could use a hike, too."

Brenna dashed to us and rocked onto the balls of her feet several times. "Hiking? Can I go? Can I go? Pretty please? You're going up there," she said as she raised her eyebrows, "right?"

I swore she was going to give us away.

Aaren gave her a warning look, then said, "Of course you can come."

She jumped up and down until Aaren knelt by her and whispered, "But you can't hike *too* high up the mountain, you know. Not until you are ten, like we were."

Brenna's face fell. Two days before the quakes, she'd turned six. "B-but . . . ," she stammered. "But you let me go before!"

"Shh, Brenna." I glanced around to make sure Jella's family couldn't hear us.

"Only when it was more dangerous to *not* go," Aaren said. "Right now, it's not. You'll have to wait."

During the walk toward the orchards, I wondered how long it would take to get things back to normal. Even with everyone working from sunup to sundown, I imagined it could be months before we got to the last damaged building or road.

It took thirty minutes to walk, run, and hike up the mountain to our spot right below the Bomb's Breath and would take another thirty minutes to get back, so we had an hour at the very most to sky jump. I could barely stand that it took us so long to get there. With the deep snows and then the mud from the spring melt, we hadn't sky jumped since the bandits were here four months ago.

I could tell Aaren was beginning to feel as if it was a mistake, though. Brenna hadn't stopped trying to talk him into letting her jump the entire time.

"I'm only trying to keep you safe!" Aaren said.

Brenna folded her arms. "I went through it when I was sick and I stayed safe then. I can do it, Aaren! I can!"

"I'll make you a deal," Aaren said. "I'll work with you on holding your breath for a long time all summer. When you can do it while I sing the 'Happy Birthday' song three times, even if I try to startle you, then I'll let you jump. Deal?"

I didn't think Brenna would've smiled any bigger if Aaren had told her that he was going to make her wings so she could fly. Which, I guess, is kind of what he promised her.

"I'll stay with her first," Brock offered.

"Really?" Aaren said. "Thanks!"

Aaren and I waved our arms as we hiked up the mountainside, feeling for the dense air that made up the Bomb's Breath—the band of air that nobody but the three of us dared go through, because everyone in White Rock knew how easily it could kill us. We inhaled, then hurried up the mountainside and through the Bomb's Breath, careful not to breathe while in the middle of it. When we reached the boulder that told us we were beyond the danger, we gulped air.

My long hair was already pulled into a ponytail, but I braided it to keep it a little more contained, then pulled a band out of my pocket and wound it around the end. Aaren pushed his blond curls off his forehead—not that they were going to stay that way for long.

"We're out of practice," he said.

"Yep. So we should probably start with something easy. Belly flop?"

He grasped my hand. "Running."

I responded by sprinting with him along the narrow face of the lower cliff until we reached our normal sky-jumping spot. I looked at Aaren to make sure he was ready. He nodded, and we took a huge breath and flung ourselves off the edge of the cliff.

The lower cliff was a foot or two above the Breath, so we only free-fell for a moment before we plunged into the compressed air. It felt as if time stopped. Gravity went away. Earthquake damage seemed to disappear. Every care in the world floated somewhere above or below the Bomb's Breath, and all that was left inside it was me flying. Me, lying facedown, seeing the cliff base, where Brock and Brenna stood below, as we drifted closer.

I held my free hand up, then flipped it over. That was our cue to try a trick we had worked on for months last summer. We slowly moved our clasped hands downward, then flung them above our heads. The momentum yanked us onto our backs, and I stared up at the white fluffy clouds, imagining I floated on one of them. If I didn't have to breathe soon, and if I wasn't sinking closer and closer to the bottom of the Breath, I could stay here forever. Floating. Escaping.

We squirmed around until we got in a crouching position, with our feet toward the cliff below. I enjoyed every last second until I fell out of the Breath and hit the ground with a thump. All was right with the world. All was right everywhere.

We took turns being the one at the base of the cliff with Brenna, below the Bomb's Breath. It had been so long since any of us had jumped, we raced up the mountainside to do our next jump faster than ever, waving our arms above us to feel for the compressed air as we ran. It didn't take long before we tried doing flips. I even attempted a double front flip from the higher cliff like I had last fall, but I was too out of practice and ended up in a headfirst dive. I had a hard time holding my breath instead of laughing at my lack of skill on the jump.

"At least we're landing better," Aaren said.

"Speak for yourself," Brock said. "I've been landing better the entire time."

Forty-five minutes into our jump time, I was taking a turn with Brenna at the base when I noticed a dead chipmunk on the mountainside. I couldn't believe I hadn't seen it earlier—it lay on the side of the cliff, a little higher than eye level. It was right by the path, too, but a rock next to it kind of hid it. I hoped Brenna hadn't seen it. Animals walked up into the Bomb's Breath all the time, and it killed them as easily as it could kill us. It always made Brenna so sad. I pointed to Brock and Aaren, almost to the top of the upper cliff, and told Brenna to keep a close eye on them. I went to nudge the chipmunk with a stick to get it out of Brenna's sight.

When I got closer to it, I noticed the line we had drawn with a rock on the cliff face last year that showed where the Bomb's Breath began. The chipmunk was below it. By almost a foot.

I scooted in for a closer look, but the chipmunk wasn't covered with dirt as though it had rolled down the hill. It looked like it had died exactly where it was. I reached my hand up to feel the compressed air of the Bomb's Breath. Aaren's and Brock's excited squeals filled the air at the same time panic attacked my insides.

"Hope!" Brenna called. "Come watch! You missed their flips!"

I rushed back to Brenna as Brock and Aaren drifted out of the Bomb's Breath and dropped to the ground.

As soon as Aaren noticed my face, he said, "What's wrong?"

I wasn't even sure I could talk, but somehow I managed to say, "I think the Bomb's Breath lowered."

# Dropping

Aaren reached his hand up and moved it back and forth. "The Breath's just above my head here. It's never been this close! Why didn't we notice?"

"We were having too much fun," Brock said.

"And we felt for the Breath as we went up the hill each time," I said. "If we hadn't—if we had gone off our marking on the cliff instead—"

Brenna finished my sentence for me, a horrified look on her face. "You could've taken a breath too late and died!"

"We always take a breath early," Aaren said. "We'd have been okay."

Brock looked across the hazy air in the valley, his eyes settling on the part of the mountainside with the wide crevices. "Do you think maybe the Bomb's Breath hasn't moved, but the earthquake just changed things enough that the mountain is in a different spot?"

Aaren shook his head. "An earthquake capable of that wouldn't have left a single building standing in White Rock. It's something else. We need to tell someone. Hope, we have to tell your dad."

As much as I dreaded telling my dad that, once again, I had been jumping into the Bomb's Breath, I knew we had to. The gnawing pit in my stomach told me this was serious.

"Is it still lowering?" Brock said. "If it dropped a foot because of an earthquake, it's not a huge deal—everything's far enough away from it. If it's *still* dropping, that's a whole lot worse."

We stayed silent as that sank in. Or maybe we did because we couldn't bear to say how bad that would be out loud. Well, all of us but Brenna.

"The Bomb's Breath is going to come down by our houses?" she asked. "We could jump off our roofs into it!" Then she spun toward the livestock farms on the fourth ring. "Oh, but the cows! What will they do? Is it going to kill the cows?"

She looked up at Aaren with big concerned eyes, and he whispered, "No. Everything will be fine."

26

"We need to figure out if it's still dropping before we cause a panic," Brock said.

Aaren walked over to our mark on the cliff face, picked up a rock, and waved his hand to see where the compressed air started. He drew a new line with the rock, then felt the air again and again to make sure his line was at exactly the right place. "We'll come back tomorrow. When it's time to leave home in the morning to go help the Johnsons, we'll come here first. See if the Bomb's Breath is any lower. Then we'll tell your dad, Hope."

The next morning, Brock, Aaren, Brenna, and I raced across the orchards as the sun was peeking over the top of the crater.

"Plan?" Brock asked, huffing.

"If the Breath *hasn't* moved, then everything is okay, and we can go to the Johnsons' and tell my dad tonight," I said. "If we hurry, we might get there at the right time. If it *has* lowered . . ." I took a deep breath. "Everything's not okay, and we'll take the nine a.m. train to my dad at the mill."

No one even asked about that part of my plan. They were probably hoping it wouldn't matter. After all, it's not as if the Breath would continue to lower. It had never done that. It just lowered one time because of the quakes. An anomaly. And like Brock said, everyone stayed far enough away that a foot wasn't going to make too much of a difference. The warning fences were at the back edge of the fourth ring, and the bottom of the Bomb's Breath was forty feet higher. And that was if you went straight up. If you hiked the mountainside, you had to climb several hundred feet to reach it. The fact that it dropped a foot wouldn't make a difference at all.

We climbed over the warning fences and up our path to the cliff face where Aaren had marked the Bomb's Breath. I squeezed Brenna's hand tight. Aaren waved his arm in the Breath over and over, and none of us breathed.

Finally, he picked up a rock and scratched a line on the cliff face. It was a full two inches lower than the line he had scratched yesterday afternoon.

No one moved.

"It's only two inches," Brock said. "That's not too bad—right?"

Aaren didn't take his eyes off the mark.

Brenna looked up at Aaren. "So it's getting lower? It's going to keep coming down?"

I looked out across my valley. At all the homes and shops and farms and buildings my town had spent forty years building. This was the only crater left behind by the bombs for hundreds and hundreds of miles—it's not as though there was another one we could move into. Without it, we wouldn't be sheltered from bandits or the high winds that whip across the Forbidden Flats. We'd have to walk away from everything if the Bomb's Breath lowered.

I kept my eyes on the valley while I answered her. "No, Brenna. We're going to find my dad and he'll tell Mr. Hudson, and they'll fix it. What time is it, Aaren?"

"Eight forty-five."

"We need to get on a train to reach my dad, and the last one before dinnertime leaves City Circle at nine a.m. We have to make it!"

We raced down the path to the warning fences and ran to the grain tram at the edge of the orchard. We pulled the platform to us and climbed on, our weight sending the platform soaring down the tram path at a high enough speed that it rocked back and forth. I scrambled to the brakes, slowing the platform only enough to keep us from flying out of it.

The wind rushed past us, whipping my hair and making my eyes sting. We had barely passed the pole at the top of the third ring when the steam whistle at City Circle blew, signaling five minutes before the trains traveled up their tracks. Five minutes to make it a mile and a half.

I let my foot off the brake, and the fields flew past us in a blur. When we started swinging a little too much, I put the brake on a bit. Once I could see the end pole, I pressed on the brake even more. We came to a skidding stop three feet before the end pole. Perfect timing on the brakes, if you asked me.

We leapt out of the tram and dashed alongside the ditch that circled the ring of shops around City Circle. If it hadn't been full of water, we'd have run in the ditch to avoid all the weeds and rocks along the bank. We were still a hundred feet away when the whistle blew, telling the trains to go.

"No!" Brock yelled.

The conductor looked back and waved for us to hurry as the train began slowly moving forward on the repaired track. Steam billowed in a cloud from the small car at the front where the conductor stood, and drifted across the two open-topped passenger cars it pulled farther and farther up the hill. Aaren and Brock picked up Brenna, and I raced alongside the train, pumping my legs as the wheels on the side of the end car inched closer and closer. Finally, I got near enough to leap onto the passenger car. I reached back for Brenna, pulling her next to me right before Brock and Aaren both jumped up beside us. We collapsed onto a bench.

"I can't believe we made it," Aaren said.

Brock panted. "I can't believe Hope didn't kill us."

Brenna looked up at me with her big blue eyes. "Can we do it again?"

My heart rate and breathing had barely returned to normal when the train reached the river at the top of the third ring, its final stop.

We hopped off and headed straight for the mill on the edge of the river. The double doors were open, letting in the cool spring air, and we could hear the sounds coming from the mill over the chugging of the train.

As soon as we walked in the doors, heat from the wood-drying kiln hit us, along with the *chonk* and *bang* from the nail-making machine and the whirring of the saws. When my dad noticed us, he shut down the saw, pulled out his earplugs, and took off his safety glasses.

"Hey, pumpkin. What's wrong?"

# The Falling Sky

My dad told us not to talk to a soul about what we had found until Mr. Hudson figured out what was going on, because he didn't want to panic anyone before he had answers. After a very long three and a half days, Mr. Hudson asked my dad, Brock, Aaren, and me to join him in the clearing by the woods on the second ring, right next to the cracks in the earth.

The sun had just sunk behind the crater, and Mr. Hudson already had lanterns lit, shining light on the two tables he had hauled up from his workshop. They were covered from one end to the other in piles of papers, glass beakers, a gas burner, a lantern, mortars and pestles, and a microscope. Off to the side, a bedroll and pillow lay, but it didn't look as if Mr. Hudson had used them for a while. His hair was a mess, his clothes were wrinkled, and he had dark circles under his eyes. A chair sat next to one of the tables, but he stood, leaning over some charts. We climbed off our horses and he looked up at us with tired eyes.

"So they were right?" my dad said. "It's lowering?"

Mr. Hudson gave a single nod.

My dad walked to the same side of the table as Mr. Hudson and in a quiet voice asked, "How much?"

Mr. Hudson ran his hand through his dark hair, making it stick up even worse than it was already, then pulled his black case toward him. The one I'd seen him carry a million times. Lots of things changed when the green bombs hit, including minerals, ores, and plants. Right after the bombs, when Mr. Hudson was my age, he traveled with his parents and my grandparents from Holyoke, Colorado, across the Forbidden Flats, picking up other survivors along the way. They were the original members of White Rock, back before they'd even found White Rock. He began collecting samples of the minerals and metals he found on that trip, as well as every excursion they'd gone on since then to scavenge for supplies. He brought them all back, performed tests, categorized them, and found each a spot in his black case.

He pulled a sheet of paper out of his stack that had

been torn from a book. Aaren, Brock, and I crowded around the table to see it—the periodic table of elements, with notes added in his own handwriting.

He used two fingers to tap on the chart. "Chemical reactions don't only happen with liquids. They can happen with solids." Mr. Hudson looked at Aaren, Brock, and me. "Remember in Tens and Elevens, when I showed you a double replacement?"

I nodded. "You put two white powders in the same vial, and when you mixed them together, they turned yellow, right?"

Mr. Hudson smiled at me as though he was impressed that I had been paying attention enough in inventions class to remember that. "Right. Because it underwent a chemical change." He motioned behind him toward the giant cracks that looked like claw marks in the ground. "The same type of thing happened in these fissures, only with different elements."

Mr. Hudson pulled two stones out of his black case. He held up the first one, a rounded stone so dark gray it was almost black, then the second stone, one with jagged edges that was at least as dark but had a purplish shine to it. "Neither of these existed before the bombs. There are seams of both of these in this mountain, running almost parallel."

Using a chisel, he broke a piece off each stone and put each in its own mortar. He handed one mortar to Aaren, and they both ground their stone into a powder with the pestles.

He held them out for us to see, as if he were teaching us a class back in Tens & Elevens. "See? Separate elements. But when I combine them . . ." He poured them both into a vial, then put the stopper on the vial and shook it a few times.

A light gray powder filled the bottom of the vial, but slow-moving, almost see-through smoke filled the rest of the container.

"A double replacement. The chemical change did two things—one made the color you see in the bottom, the other created a gas." He pulled off the stopper, and the gas lazily drifted out of the vial. "You can see the gas better when it's in the vial, because it's concentrated. Even though you can't see it once it leaves the vial, it's still rising.

"The shaking of the quakes crashed the seams of both these minerals together, turning much of the minerals into powder and mixing them." He gazed at the sky. "This gas is traveling upward, combining with the gases in the Bomb's Breath, and making it . . . heavier, in a sense."

I looked up at the few stars that were beginning to shine in the darkening sky. I couldn't see the Bomb's

Breath, of course, and from where I stood on the second ring, I was probably eighty or ninety feet below it. Or at least that's how high up it was before it started lowering. The thought was suffocating.

"Is it only happening here?" my dad asked.

"Yes," Mr. Hudson said. "That's the first thing I worried about, too. I marked the level of the Bomb's Breath on the outside of the crater and checked it the next day. It is staying at the same height it always has. It's only coming down within White Rock, and it's not pulling the rest down with it. It'll stay fifteen feet thick, too—the entire thing will just drop lower and lower. The more of this gas that travels up to the Bomb's Breath, the more the Bomb's Breath will descend on us. This is a sustained chemical change, so it will continue to create the gas for weeks."

"*Weeks?*" my dad said, his voice urgent.

"Yes. About eight weeks, in fact." Mr. Hudson fumbled with the mess of papers on his table and pulled out one with mathematical equations on it. "But we'll never make it eight weeks, because the problem is compounding. The Bomb's Breath lowered roughly two and a half inches in the past day, but in a week, it'll be dropping seven inches in a day. In three weeks, seventy-two inches a day. It will drop to the highest houses on the third ring in twenty-three days."

Aaren's and my houses, along with a handful of others and the tunnel leading out of White Rock, were the highest on the third ring. I wasn't sure my legs could hold me up. *Twenty-three days. Twenty-three days. Twenty-three days.* My heart pounded to the rhythm of the only words surging through my brain.

"Can't we fill in the cracks with dirt?" I asked. "Cover them up so the gases won't come out?"

"That won't stop the gases—they'll still seep right through the dirt." Mr. Hudson waved his arm toward the sky. "That hazy air we've been seeing—it's caused by those gases. When it combines with the particles in the Bomb's Breath, the particles turn gray. The haze will continue to get worse until we can fix it."

"So there's a way to fix it?" My dad's voice came out hoarse.

The black case lay open on the table, and Mr. Hudson gestured to the rows and rows of items contained in it. Hundreds of rocks of different shapes, sizes, colors, and textures filled the bottom half of the case, some of them shining as if they were made of metal, and others as dull as dirt. The top half of the case held dozens of vials filled with different-colored powders and liquids.

"I think there is. I've tested all of these, and there is one that stops the gases from being created, and should allow the Bomb's Breath to go back up to its natural height." Mr. Hudson pulled a rock out of his case. "Seforium."

I had never seen a stone like it before. It was a rich orange color and was nearly as chalky as limestone.

Optimism flashed across my dad's face. "It'll stop it?"

"It will."

"Where can we find it? We can put a hold on rebuilding and get as many people as you need to mine it."

Mr. Hudson set the orange rock on the table and faced my dad, his eyes looking older in the flickering light from the lanterns. "I've seen it only once, and never again since. Forty years ago, not long after the bombs hit, I dug this out of the Rocky Mountains."

"The Rocky Mountains," my dad echoed.

Mr. Hudson gave a single nod.

"Five hundred miles to the west, across the Forbidden Flats?"

"If we don't get it," Mr. Hudson said, "we'll have to evacuate White Rock, or we'll be trapped in the lower rings, with the Bomb's Breath coming down on us."

# Emergency Meeting

It was late by the time my dad got everyone in the council gathered for a meeting in my kitchen to discuss an expedition to the Rocky Mountains. I pretended to go to bed and listened from the hallway.

They debated whether they should send a large group so they could better fight off any bandits they came across, or take a small group so they could travel quickly. They decided that with as little time as we had, they didn't have a choice—they'd better send a small group and do it fast. Then they discussed who to send on the trip, what to take, how to travel quickly, how hard it might be to find a seam of seforium, and how long it could take to mine it. They talked for a long time about the dangers they'd face until my head spun and my stomach churned. I finally gave up listening and went to bed.

I fell asleep and dreamed I sat on the flat part of the roof on the community center, and instead of being see-through, the Bomb's Breath was an intense orange, like sunset on an angry sky. On all sides of me, people scurried around doing things, but I sat on the roof, watching the Bomb's Breath lower. I wanted to help, too, but I couldn't move. Instead, I watched as it sank into the third ring, swallowing my house with its darkness. People dropped to the ground whenever it touched them. Lower and lower still, and I just sat on the roof in the lowest part of White Rock, not doing anything. It descended to the second ring, and then the first, and still I sat, watching people fall to the ground all around me. When it came down enough to almost swallow me, I woke with a scream, shaking.

And then I realized it wasn't only my scream that awoke me—it was also the scream of the steam whistle at City Circle, blowing three short whistles, three long whistles, then three short whistles: the signal that we'd have an emergency town meeting in one hour. I jumped out of bed and hurried to the kitchen to ask my parents about it, but they were both gone.

I picked up a note on my kitchen table in my mom's handwriting.

*We had to leave early for the community center. Take the 8:00 a.m. train down to meet us.*

The train wouldn't be here for almost an hour—I couldn't sit around waiting for that long when I was so rattled. I got ready as quickly as possible, then went next door and knocked for Aaren, and we both jogged down to the community center. It was already pretty crowded. Everyone who had arrived early went from classroom to classroom to gather chairs and benches and set them up in the gym. The high windows on the angled part of the roof wouldn't be replaced for a while, but at least the broken glass on the floor had been swept up. Aaren saw Brock come in and they both started helping with the chairs, but I went into the kitchens. I needed my mom.

She was pressing a ball of biscuit dough flat on the counter and directing a group of people putting together breakfast sandwiches. When she saw me, she wiped her hands on a towel and wrapped arms around me that weren't as bony as they once were. In fact, she felt stronger every day. I would never have guessed that my mom would've changed so much from bandits invading months before.

She whispered, "Are you okay?"

Those words coming from her made me realize how

much I wasn't okay, especially after the nightmare that awoke me. I nodded anyway. It was a minute before I trusted my voice to come out normal. "I'm fine. Need any help?"

She looked at the flurry of activity in the kitchen. "Of course! Your dad decided it would be better to feed everyone, so they can get straight back to work after the meeting instead of sticking around and worrying. With your help, we can get these finished in time to find a seat."

I assembled sandwiches until people from the trains started filing into the gym. My mom took off her apron and walked with me through the crowd, to the spot on the front row of benches where she always sat.

Usually Aaren, Brock, Brenna, and I stood toward the back, so we could see everyone's reactions. Today, though, I wanted to be by my mom. We sat there, knowing why an emergency meeting was called, while all the people around us were trying to guess.

Eventually, the five council members walked in and took their seats on the raised platform at the front. The noise from the crowd cut in half, but everyone shifted in their seats, looking toward the doors for my dad.

A few moments later, he came into the gym holding his clipboard, looking in charge and confident even while limping to the front to step up onto the platform.

He leaned against the table and looked out into the crowd.

The room was packed, with all the chairs and benches taken, yet there were still more people standing than there were sitting.

My dad cleared his throat. "Let's get right to this. I trust everyone to remain calm and quiet while I explain." He looked at us like he was trying to judge how we'd take the news. "You've all noticed the massive fissures in the mountainside on the west. We've found out there are gases being released from within them. The gases aren't poisonous. They are, however, rising to mix with the air in the Bomb's Breath." My dad took a long pause. "And that's making the Bomb's Breath lower."

The noise level in the room rose so much, I thought maybe my dad had been too quick to trust us to remain calm and quiet. But he stood there, patiently waiting for the noise to die down. He'd told me once that people would be quiet on their own quickly enough, when their need to hear information became stronger than their need to talk. This time, it happened really fast.

"The good news is, there's a mineral that will stop the gases," he said, and the entire room held their breath as they waited for the *but*. "But as far as we know, it is only found in the Rocky Mountains."

Everyone gasped.

"We'll need to send a team tomorrow morning to travel across the Forbidden Flats to get the mineral. Ken Williams," my dad said, and he motioned behind him, "will lead the team, and those joining him will be notified soon.

"Yes, it's a long trip. And yes, it will be dangerous. We don't know much about the weather or where bandits and any towns are, so we are hoping to go with a guide. We have reports that there's someone in Arris who has been to the Rockies. Two of our men left at first light to see if the man will guide us, and they should be back by tonight. If he can't, we still leave in the morning. We have no time to waste."

My dad looked out across the crowd for a moment before continuing. "I'm going to trust you with the whole truth, because I think you deserve it, but I'm also trusting you not to panic." He paused for a minute. "We now have twenty-two days to get the mineral and be back, or the Bomb's Breath will be low enough to affect homes. That's not long to travel so far. But we've gotten through some pretty tough times before, and we'll do it again."

# The Guide

It was hard to go back and rebuild houses after the meeting. I understood the need to keep busy, but I wondered if it was all pointless. If they couldn't find the mineral or make it back in time and the Bomb's Breath kept coming down, would each family go find another town to live in? Would we all go somewhere together? I couldn't imagine another twenty-one days of wondering if they'd make it back before the Bomb's Breath engulfed my house.

We used chisels to remove mortar from the bricks that had fallen off the broken part of the Johnsons' house. I picked up a hammer and chisel and added my *clang, clang, crack!* to the clamor of everyone else's, wishing the noise would drown out my dad's words. The only thing able to do that, though, seemed to be my dream, which kept replaying in my head. The one where I sat and did nothing to help.

I stared up at the sky. Was the haze getting worse? It was hard to tell.

Aaren, Brenna, and I trudged home from the five p.m. train. As we neared my house, my exhaustion vanished when I heard horses. Four of them were picketed by the shed.

"They're here!" We ran to the house, and the three of us burst through the front door.

My mom came into the room and took my jacket off me like I was two years old, hanging it on the coatrack. "The man who's been to the Rockies hasn't agreed to be our guide yet, but he's staying for dinner so we can discuss it."

"Me too?" I asked hopefully.

My mom smiled and said yes.

"And Aaren?" I asked, brushing mortar powder from my shirt.

"If it's okay with his mom," she said. "Aaren, you take Brenna home and get cleaned up, then if you can, come back and join us. Hope, you better get cleaned up, too."

I headed to my room, sounds of talking drifting toward me from the kitchen. I probably should've taken a bath, but instead, I just changed clothes and washed my face, arms, and hands, then took out my braid and tried to brush the little chunks of mortar from it.

Aaren must've done about the same, because I heard his soft knock on the kitchen door when I walked down the hallway.

I came around the corner into my kitchen, and saw my parents, Mr. Hudson, Mr. Williams, Aaren's dad, and a man I didn't know at the table. Aaren and I slipped into the two empty seats at the end of one of the sides.

"Hey, pumpkin," my dad said.

I almost ducked when all eyes focused on me. "Hi, Dad."

"Luke, this is my daughter, Hope, and her friend Aaren. Hope and Aaren, this is Luke Strickland. We've already offered him wealth and compliments. Right now, we are making friendly conversation in hopes that we will endear ourselves to him enough that he'll agree to be our guide." My dad winked, and everyone laughed at his candor.

Luke tipped his head at us. I gave him a polite smile as my dad got up and helped my mom place steaming platters of potatoes, roast beef, gravy, and green beans in the middle of the table.

I kept staring at the man while the adults talked. His hair was dark, thick, and cut short. I knew I'd never seen him before, but for some reason, he looked familiar. Not as though I knew him exactly; more like he reminded me of someone.

Once my parents sat down, Mr. Williams said, "Tell us about the trail between here and the Rockies."

Luke snorted. "Well, for starters, there isn't a 'trail.' More like open space, gullies, unpredictable weather, bandits, and infrequent towns. It's a fairly straight shot from here, though, and White Rock River will be at your right for most of your journey. Your best chance to get past bandits without too much trouble is if you take as few people as possible. Bigger groups tend to attract them more. Then get the best horses around and make the trip on horseback. You could get there in seven or eight days."

My dad shook his head. "We'll take a small group, and we do have the best horses, but we'll need to take a trailer."

"Not as safe," Luke said, "and it'll take you probably twice as long that way."

I did the math in my head. Twice that long there and twice that long back meant somewhere between twenty-four and twenty-eight days, plus however long it took to find and mine the seforium. I looked at my dad in alarm, and he looked at Luke.

"We only have twenty-one days."

Luke cut a few pieces of his meat. "If luck goes with

you, there's a chance you can make it. Not a great chance, but a chance." He narrowed his eyes at my dad. "Mind telling me what kind of cargo you're planning on that requires a trailer?"

Mr. Hudson glanced at my dad and my dad gave him a small nod. "This," he said as he pulled the orange stone from his jacket pocket. "I'm sure you saw the fissures on the side of the mountain on your way into White Rock?"

"Hard to miss," Luke said.

"In powder form, this will counteract the gases being released from those fissures that are causing the Bomb's Breath to lower. Within a few weeks, it will lower to the height of our homes. A few days after that, it will have dropped to the height of the fissures, making White Rock unlivable."

Luke studied Mr. Hudson and the stone, as though he was calculating something. "There's a town at the Rockies—Heaven's Reach—that mines all kinds of minerals. They're self-sufficient so they don't need many supplies, and they aren't trusting of strangers, but if you negotiate well, they might make a trade. If you can pay, that could save you some time."

Everyone seemed to let out a breath of relief at the same time. They might not need to search for the seforium, or worry that they couldn't find it or mine it quickly enough!

"We can pay," my dad said.

Aaren leaned in close and whispered, "I bet he's talking about the Ameiphus! My mom's been working on getting the last few batches finished."

"Good," Luke said. "There's also a trading town along the way—Glacier City—where you can buy feed for your horses on the way there and the way back, so you won't have to carry so much extra weight. It'll help you to travel more quickly."

"Good to know," my dad said.

Luke dug into his potatoes. He seemed to be deep in thought, and no one talked.

After a minute or two that seemed like an eternity, my dad said, "We have twenty-one days from tomorrow morning. Will you help us?"

"It's dangerous."

My dad didn't take his eyes off Luke. "We'll pay you well."

Everyone around the table leaned in, concerned and hopeful looks on their faces.

"There's something you should know about the place with the minerals," Luke said. "The entire town of Heaven's Reach resides *above* the air of the Bomb's Breath."

"What?" my dad said. "You can't be serious!"

Luke shrugged.

I focused on Mr. Williams, who had turned pale. He was the only one going from the council, so he would be handling negotiations with whoever was in charge at Heaven's Reach. My dad would never make anyone go anywhere near the Bomb's Breath, though, and after Mr. Williams's dog, Sandy, died in the Bomb's Breath a few months ago, he would especially never make Mr. Williams go.

My dad's forehead crinkled. "But how do they—"

"They have some kind of device that they wear that allows them to pass through the Bomb's Breath without dying, but I've never seen one for sale."

"Will they come down to trade?" my dad asked.

Luke shrugged. "Maybe. I've seen the mayor and others from their town, and even traded with them. There's just no way to let them know to come down to talk with you. It definitely could be faster to get the seforium from them than to find it yourself. But as likely as not, you'll have to wait weeks for them to happen to come down. Going there to get the seforium might be a much faster option, or it could make you lose a lot of time. Hard to say."

I opened my mouth, and my words came out as a croak: "I could go."

# A Chance to Go

I cleared my throat, then repeated, "I could go." I swear I hadn't even considered going before I opened my mouth, especially after listening to last night's council meeting and hearing about how dangerous the trip would be. But then I thought of my dream where I did nothing, and added, "Then you'll have someone to go through the Bomb's Breath to get the mayor."

Luke gave me a strange look—somewhere between curiosity and awe. Something I wasn't used to seeing when I talked about going through the Bomb's Breath. "If you've got someone who'll go through the Bomb's Breath, then your group has a chance and I'll be your guide. If she really can, that'd keep everyone from having to wait until the people of Heaven's Reach needed to come down on their own."

I nodded my head, feeling more and more like I *had* to go with every second that passed.

My dad crossed his arms. "No."

"She could go up as soon as you got there," Luke said. "Let the mayor know that you need him to come down and negotiate a trade. Cut out all the waiting."

"No," my dad repeated. "I'm not sending my child into danger."

"There's danger *here*, Dad! And no one in the group will go through the Bomb's Breath, but I will. I want to, and you need me to go. Everyone will keep me safe." I was sure there were other things I should say to talk him into it, but I couldn't think what they might be. All I knew was that I had to go. I couldn't stay here and not help when they needed me.

"We will," Mr. Williams said.

"I'll protect her with my life," Aaren's dad said. "We all will."

Mr. Hudson cleared his throat. "I'm not thrilled about sending a child, either. But if there's a better chance the team can get the seforium if Hope will go through the

Bomb's Breath and up to Heaven's Reach, I think we need to entertain that idea. If we don't succeed, we lose everything."

Goose bumps started on my head and rushed down my back and arms. "Please? I need to do this."

"And I could go, too," Aaren said. "Then she wouldn't have to be the only kid going."

There was a long silence.

The moment my dad opened his mouth to speak, I could tell that his answer was going to be no. But before he got a chance, in a quiet voice, my mom spoke. "David, I think we should let her go."

My dad stared at my mom for a long moment, then walked out the back door, letting it slam behind him. I stood up when I heard my dad's heavy boots clomp down the wooden stairs to the yard.

My mom glanced at the door. "I think he needs a minute alone."

I looked around the table at all the eyes that were on me. Giving me looks full of questions and worry and pity and expectations. I took that as my cue to leave. "Excuse me," I mumbled. I gave Aaren's sleeve a little tug, then headed for the front porch.

Aaren and I sat and watched as the sun set behind the crater, throwing brilliant colors across the sky. I stared at the way the trees became silhouettes, their new leaves sprouting into the sunset.

"Are you sure you want to go?" Aaren's voice was soft, but still made me jump. "It sounds pretty scary."

Images from my dream flashed into my mind, reminding me how terrible it felt to not do anything while the Bomb's Breath came down. Now that there was a chance I might help, there was no way I could stay here. "Yes, I'm sure."

"Because you want to get out of rebuilding houses?"

I surprised myself and laughed.

"Oh, wait. No—you're afraid that school will start again, and you're trying to miss out on inventions class."

I laughed again and punched him in the arm.

"You know, they could make you ride in a cramped trailer the whole way. Or walk the whole way. Or they might give you a horse, but it'll be Chance."

"You volunteered to go, too. Are you sure *you* want to go?"

"Of course!" He bit his lip. "If I can talk my parents into it."

I bumped my shoulder into his. "They said this trip could be dangerous. So we probably need someone who knows about being a doctor."

He grinned.

"You go work on your parents. I'll work on my dad."

* * *

When I found my dad, he was leaning against the wooden fence that separated the backyard from the fields, staring out over sprouting carrot tops colored a weird shade of orange from the remnants of the sunset.

"I'm not afraid," I said.

"I *can't* go." His voice was almost pleading. "This town needs a leader now more than ever, but still, I'd leave everything that needs to be done to someone else. I'd go with you in a heartbeat if it meant keeping you safe. But this leg—" He gestured with both hands to the spot where Mickelson shot him four months ago. "I couldn't make it five miles on a horse, let alone five hundred. I can't keep you safe unless you stay here."

"Nowhere is perfectly safe, Dad. Not even here. *Especially* not here. If I don't go, then here might be the most dangerous place there is. Sometimes you have to take a risk."

"Sometimes I think you're too much like me." My dad sighed. "And sometimes I think we're nothing alike. I've never been as daring as you are. Your willingness, your bravery . . . It still doesn't make it easy to let you leave, you know."

"But we *have* to get the mineral in time."

My dad dropped his head and stared at the wooden plank that formed the top of the fence for a long time.

I looked across the fields as the last bits of dusk faded away.

"Let's go in," my dad said. "The expedition leaves in the morning whether we're ready for it or not."

"Sorry about the bumps," Aaren's dad said from my favorite horse Arabelle's back. "This road took more damage than we thought."

In the predawn light, the open cart rocked back and forth as Arabelle pulled it along the third ring road, headed to the clearing by the tunnel opening. She wasn't moving very fast, so Aaren and I left my parents sitting in it with our luggage and jumped out. After the stress of trying to talk my parents into letting me go, our rush to get everything packed, and people continuing to come over to our house long after I had finally gotten to bed, I was edgy.

Aaren's dad pulled Arabelle to a stop at the tunnel opening, near a trailer and a dozen people making preparations for the group to leave. I grabbed my bags and trotted ahead.

The trailer we were taking was one we almost never used in White Rock, but they always used it on scavenging runs or to trade with another town. It was a big, sturdy rectangular box on wheels, with doors at the back that opened as wide as the trailer.

Mr. Williams marked things off a checklist as he directed everyone in rearranging the gear in the trailer. Aaren and I handed his older brother Cole and Mr. Williams's daughter Cass our bags, and they put them in with all the rest.

Luke walked up to me and my parents. "Morning. I assume you have the Ameiphus you plan to use as payment well hidden?"

"We do," my dad said. "Seven hundred doses, with fifty of them in a smaller bag, in case a trade along the way is needed." Then he turned to me. "You can still say no. You don't have to go."

"Dad," I said, "I'll be fine."

Then his eyes shifted to something away from me, and he said, "Brock?"

I whirled around and saw Brock at the back of the trailer with his arms full of supplies.

"Brock!" I called out. "Are you going with us?" After how hard it was for Aaren and me to talk our parents into letting us go, I didn't think there was a chance in the world that Brock would also be able to go.

My dad raised his eyebrows at Mr. Williams. "Please tell me he's only here to help load things."

"Well, not exactly," Mr. Williams said. "The kid's determined to go. Mark my words—if we leave him behind, he'll find a way to sneak out and join us. I figured if we take him, we can keep him safer than if he's by himself, trying to catch up with us."

"Brock," my dad called out, then motioned for him to come over. "Why do you want to go so badly?"

Brock shrugged. "White Rock helped me and my family." Then he glanced at Aaren and me. "And friends look out for each other."

My dad studied him for a moment. I hoped he was thinking that it would be cruel to tell Brock no when both Aaren and I were going. And that it wouldn't be right if it wasn't all three of us. "Is your mom okay with this?"

"She's okay enough."

My dad rubbed his hand across his forehead.

"We'll keep the kids out of harm's way," Mr. Williams said.

My dad shook his head as though he wasn't comfortable with any of the three of us going, but he turned to Mr. Williams anyway. "Everything ready?"

Mr. Williams said he thought so, and they walked to

the trailer to make a last-minute check. Brock took that as permission to go, and the three of us picked up the remaining bags from the cart and loaded them into the trailer before we walked back to my mom.

When it was time to say goodbye, my dad limped over to us. "Be safe."

"Three weeks is a long time," my mom said.

I had only slept outside of White Rock once in my entire life—the night we'd spent in Browning when the bandits came four months ago. Three weeks sounded impossibly long.

She cocked her head. "You'll be fine, though?"

"I will."

Yes, I was sad. And a little scared. But as people started untying the horses' reins and leading them into the tunnel, an excitement crept in. I was going to see places and people and things I had never seen before. When the trailer started moving toward the tunnel, the excitement overtook the sadness. The trailer, pulled by two horses and led by Mr. Williams, made the turn into the tunnel, and Aaren's dad, Luke, Cole, and Cass walked behind it, leading the seven horses we were taking. I gave my parents one last goodbye, and then ran with Brock and Aaren to catch up as they strode past the sentry guards and into the tunnel.

When we walked through the tunnel this time, I made sure to keep my eyes off the miles of rock above us. It helped that the mountain no longer groaned. I bent toward Aaren and spoke barely loud enough to be heard over the rushing of the river. "What happened after you left last night?"

Aaren shrugged. "Big family meeting. My mom already hated that my dad and my brother Cole were going. And Cole's seven years older than me! My mom said it was too dangerous and if something bad happened, then she'd lose two kids. Then I said I should go *because* it was dangerous—the group would need a doctor. She said she really had to train someone who wasn't one of her offspring to be the backup doctor. But, eventually, they decided I could go."

"I'm glad you're here," I said. "Cole and your dad, too. What did your mom say, Brock, when you told her you wanted to come?"

Brock stared up at the tunnel ceiling for a moment, then shrugged. "I don't know—I wasn't there. I left her a note."

I gasped. "You didn't ask her?"

"What happens when she finds out?" Aaren asked.

"It won't be as bad for me as it was for you two. When my family lived in Browning and I moved to White Rock to take care of my grandpa, I lived without them for almost a year. My family can handle it."

"Yes," I said, trying to keep my voice a whispered yell instead of an actual yell. "But you were *safe* in White Rock."

"Yeah, sure I was," Brock said. "Until bandits attacked."

"Good point," I admitted.

He shrugged. "We'll be safe."

I had been so focused on our conversation, I hadn't noticed that we'd reached the end of the tunnel until I saw the sunshine on Brock's face. We were officially out of White Rock, and beginning our expedition.

# A Rocky Start

The sun hadn't risen high enough to peek over the mountain in White Rock, but as I walked into the open, I had to squint against its brightness. And there was no haze! I hadn't realized how bad it had gotten in our valley until I saw the blue sky above us.

Luke walked his horse over to me. "Incredible, isn't it?"

I nodded. The sights around us were mesmerizing. And so was the sweet scent of growing things that drifted toward us on the wind. With all the springtime grasses, the Forbidden Flats were green for miles and miles until they met the brilliant blue sky far off in the distance. In

White Rock, everything had a stopping point. The edge of the first ring. The edge of the orchards. The edges of the lake. The top edge of the crater. Out here, though, there were no edges—things went on forever and ever. The trees sprouted leaves, and some were even blossoming. The river disappeared into the tunnel behind me, but in front of me, it snaked out as far as I could see. I knew that Browning sat ten miles to our left, but I couldn't see any of its mounded dirt walls this far away.

"How many times have you been out here?" Luke asked.

I took my eyes off the Forbidden Flats for a moment to glance at him. "When I was three, but I don't remember it. Again about four months ago, when everything was covered in snow. And then on the day of the quakes."

"I've lived on the Forbidden Flats my whole life," Luke said. "Mostly northeast of here. Before you know it, you'll be sick of seeing nothing but flatness."

I doubted that.

Mr. Williams's daughter Cass, a girl who graduated Sixteens & Seventeens last year and whose split job was to take care of the horses, led a shiny black horse named Ruben over to us. "For you and Brock," she said, and held his reins while I climbed up.

Brock put his hand on Ruben's neck. "I thought there were enough for us each to ride our own."

"Nope." Cass took off her jacket and tied its arms around her waist. "They're fast, healthy horses, but we still need to have two without riders at all times to switch places with the horses pulling the trailer."

Brock climbed into the saddle with me, while Aaren climbed on a horse with his dad. Then we spurred our horses ahead, crossed the bridge, and followed the road around the southern end of our crater, into the forest.

When we came to search for Ameiphus on the day of the earthquake, we didn't use the road. Instead, we had gone up through the mountainside to find an area that hadn't already been searched by earlier parties. The last time— the only time—I had actually taken this road was when we traveled with the guard months ago, so we could sneak in through the cave where the White Rock River exited the mountain, and rescue our town. We were on this road again to do the same thing—save our town. Except this time, we were heading away from White Rock instead of to it.

The road wasn't traveled often, and it was hard to get the trailer over the bumps and tree roots and boulders that covered much of it. The pace became so slow that Aaren, Brock, and I climbed off the horses and walked.

Once we were a little away from the others, Aaren said, "So . . . your mom must've seen your note by now. What do you think she's doing?"

I half expected to see someone riding toward us to take Brock home.

"Probably saying my name like it's a curse word." Brock shrugged. "She'll get over it."

We walked along the road, jumping off the boulders and tree trunks that were causing so much trouble for the trailer ahead of us. Every so often, the trailer would get stuck on something, and we'd have to run forward and help the others lift it, being careful not to damage the mileage trackers attached to the wheels.

Each time we stopped, Cass handed off her reins, then went horse to horse, checking on them. She'd stroke their jaws, sometimes lay her cheek on their foreheads, look into their eyes, or say something to them. Then she'd remount her horse, ask her dad how much longer it would be until we reached water again, then peer around at the horses to decide if that was fine. Same thing every time.

Once while Cass was checking Cole's horse, Cass said something to him—I couldn't tell what—and he smiled and said something back. Then he reached out and tucked a curl of her light red hair behind her ear.

"How long has your brother liked Cass?" Brock asked.

"What?" Aaren said. "He doesn't like Cass."

Brock raised an eyebrow.

"He did give her that crooked half-smile," I said.

Aaren rolled his eyes. "He gives that smile to everyone. *She* might like *him*. Most girls do, but Cole would've said something if he liked her."

We traveled all day, and by the time we made it through the forest and to the place where the river exited White Rock, the sun had set, it was way past dinnertime, and everyone was hot, sweaty, and worn out from trying to maneuver the trailer through such a rough area.

Cass and I took the horses down to the river to drink while Aaren's dad, Cole, and Luke unloaded sections of fence that hung on the outside of the trailer, clamping them together to make a pen for the horses near the river. Mr. Williams started making a fire pit and gathered items for our dinner from the trailer while Brock and Aaren searched for firewood.

When we all finally gathered around the fire with the river on one side, and the trailer and the horse pen forming a wall around us, we were starving and tired. As we finished eating our vegetable stew, Luke stood up, the fire casting different parts of him in shadow or an orange glow. "We all did good today. We didn't make it as far as I'd hoped, but the terrain from here on out is fairly flat, so hopefully we'll be able to make up for the lost time."

"It's a clear enough night," Mr. Williams added, "and everyone's tired. We'll forgo setting up the tents."

We pulled our bedrolls out of the trailer and laid them by the fire, then snuggled into our blankets. Before long, we heard several people snoring, including Aaren's dad.

"Psst!" Brock whispered. "I want to show you something."

Aaren and I slipped out of our bedrolls and tiptoed with Brock toward the trailer. Along with the horses' occasional nickers, we heard whispers. We peeked around the edge of the trailer and saw Cole leaning against the horse pen with Cass. Their faces were so close together, their whispers sounded like the wind. Brock started chuckling next to me. They were going to hear him! I caught hold of his arm and pulled him and Aaren back to our bedrolls where we laughed into the fabric as quietly as we could.

"See?" Brock said. "I was right. I'm always right!"

Even in the dim light from the embers, I could see Aaren roll his eyes. "Yes, Brock. You're very astute."

"Yeah, I am." Brock leaned in closer to me and whispered, "What does *astute* mean?"

A little of my giggling returned. "It means smart. Or clever."

Aaren and I laughed, and before long, Brock started laughing, too. Then Aaren's dad rolled over and told us to go to sleep. We each lay on our backs and watched the stars. Pretty soon, Aaren's and Brock's breathing slowed, and I could tell they were falling asleep.

"I'm really glad you two came," I whispered.

# The Forbidden Flats

We ate breakfast quickly and packed up camp. Within thirty minutes, we were back to riding on the open space alongside the river, Brock and I once again sharing a horse.

Aaren's dad steered the horse he and Aaren shared next to us. "I'm surprised you're all so wide awake with how late you stayed up talking last night."

"Some of us kept talking even after we went to sleep," Brock said, eyeing Aaren.

"It's true," I said. "Do you always do medical procedures in your sleep?"

"No!" Aaren looked between us, as though he was trying to decide if we were telling the truth or messing with him. We were definitely telling the truth. I woke up several times hearing more medical terms than I'd ever heard in the clinic with Aaren's mom.

Brock waved his hand as if he was brushing away Aaren's discomfort. "At least you don't laugh in your sleep like Hope does."

"What?" I squeaked. "You're making that up."

Mr. Grenwood chuckled, and I spun my head in his direction. "He's not."

I blushed a little, then wished I could remember my dream. It must've been a good one if I was laughing enough to wake at least two people. After a minute, I gave up. None of the dream remained. Instead, I entertained myself by staring at my surroundings. I could see so far away! It was amazing how much freedom I felt with so much open space surrounding me.

By midafternoon on the third day, though, nothing around us had changed at all. I didn't want to tell Luke that he was right and I was getting sick of seeing the Forbidden Flats, but I was actually kind of sick of seeing the Forbidden Flats. I sighed for the five hundred seventeenth time.

"I thought we'd see stuff," Brock said. "*Different* stuff. Like ruins of buildings."

"Nope," Aaren's dad said. "Not this close to White Rock. A bomb that can make a crater big enough for an entire town to live in decimates everything. You have to go out at least two hundred miles before you start seeing any remains from before the bombs. And even then, they're not full cities. Only parts."

"How long will it take to get that far away?" I asked.

He shrugged. "Another few days. But we'll get to see Glacier before then."

"You aren't getting bored already, are you?" Luke rode his horse right up next to me. I didn't even realize he'd been listening.

"No—I love it," I lied.

He raised an eyebrow. He didn't believe me for a second.

"All right," I said. "Maybe it's getting a little boring."

"A *little* boring?" Brock said.

"And we are going so slow!" I complained.

Luke grinned, and that made me smile, too. He kind of looked like a kid—like he was planning something fun. Maybe he looked familiar because his expressions were so similar to those of my friends. He jerked his chin farther up the trail. "See that clump of trees?"

Brock and I nodded. They were probably a half mile up the road—five of them together at the edge of the river.

"Race you."

Luke was so cool.

"Go!" Brock yelled. He jabbed his heels into Ruben's side, and we took off galloping.

I could faintly hear Cass and Mr. Williams yell something behind me, but I wanted to win, and I loved the feeling of being totally free, the wind blowing through my hair. I held tight to Brock's waist as we bounced ahead. Luke stayed at our side the entire time, sometimes barely pulling ahead, sometimes falling a little behind.

"Faster!" I yelled to Brock over the sound of the wind blowing past us. Brock leaned against Ruben's neck, and I leaned into Brock. We flew forward. At the last moment, Luke's horse gave an extra burst of speed, and he beat us to the trees. A second later, we reached the trees, and Brock pulled back on the reins.

"That was awesome!" Brock said.

I laughed out loud. I hadn't ridden that fast on a horse for far too long. Even though we lost, the ride was exhilarating, and made the dull landscape a billion times easier to handle.

The ground we traveled on had been getting higher and higher when compared to the river, but Luke found a spot where we could carefully walk our horses down to it. While Ruben drank, I stroked his neck and told him what a great job he did. When he was finished, I led him back up to the road.

The rest of the group neared, and I was surprised how quiet they were. Instead of the usual chatting with each other, everyone just looked ahead. Except Aaren. He looked down at his horse's mane.

Cass was the first to reach us. She flung her leg over the saddle and landed on the ground with a thud. "What do you think you're doing?!"

I was too shocked to say anything. I'd never heard Cass yell before.

"These horses have to travel more distance in three weeks than a horse should ever have to. We don't even have time to stop and let them rest. Did you forget that?"

"Relax," Luke said. "We just had a little race."

"Relax?" she yelled. "If you run them like that, they'll be dead before we make it back! They're living, breathing things. I've been so careful with each and every one of them, making sure they get rotated so they can handle this journey. They don't deserve to be abused because you want 'a little race.'"

"I'm sorry, Cass," I said, and I meant it. "I . . . didn't think. I didn't know it would be bad."

Cass glared at me for a minute.

"I'm sorry, too," Brock said.

"Maybe you didn't know better," Mr. Williams said, "but Luke did."

Luke brushed some dust off his jacket. "You two are making a big deal out of nothing."

"Out of *nothing*?" Cass looked closely at my horse's eyes and mouth, and put her hand on the big pulsing vein on the side of his neck.

"Yeah. Out of nothing," Luke said. "They got time to rest and get some water while we were waiting for you. They're good as new." He looked at Brock and me, then back at Cass. "We should go. Your town's in danger. We don't want to waste any time dillydallying." Then he heeled his horse and rode ahead of the group.

Ruben had seemed to enjoy the race. He was probably pretty sick of the scenery and going the same speed, too. But I hated making Cass mad. I stayed right where I was while she checked out Ruben. Slowly, the rest of the group joined Luke, heading on the same path beside the river. As soon as most of them were moving, I said, "Cass?"

"What?"

"I really am sorry. I didn't know it would hurt them."

She scowled in Luke's direction. "I know. I'm not mad at you."

I was glad, but I didn't want her to be mad at Luke, either.

# The Necklace

Cass's yelling had caused an awkward silence among the entire group. She rode on the right of Brock and me so she could keep an eye on Ruben. Eventually, she must've decided that Ruben was fine, because her shoulders relaxed and she stopped holding her reins so tightly.

Up ahead, Luke pulled his horse to a stop and leaned toward Mr. Williams. He said something I couldn't hear, and he pointed to a small cloud of dust ahead on the horizon. Mr. Williams pulled the trailer next to a few trees at the edge of the path and stopped. Luke turned his horse around and rode back to each of us.

When he neared Brock and me, he said in a low voice, "That might be bandits up ahead. Follow me."

Luke led everyone down the small incline to the river, where the high bank would mostly hide us. Once we were all huddled next to the river, I whispered to Luke, "Are they going to attack?"

"I doubt it," he said. "We don't even know if they're bandits. They're far away, and we hid quickly. Plus, we weren't traveling fast enough to kick up much dust. The best way to stay safe on the Forbidden Flats is to take cover if you see them in the distance. Don't give them a reason to come your way, and you'll be fine."

We stayed still on our horses, our muscles tight with worry even after Luke's words. I pulled my pendant from behind my shirt and clutched it so tight, it left indents in my hand from the tiny conglomerate rocks that formed its surface. When Ruben sidestepped and snorted, I let go of it and patted his neck, telling him everything was fine.

"That's a nice necklace," Luke said. "Where'd you get it?"

I looked down at the necklace I wore every second of every day. "I've always had it."

Luke pursed his lips and stared at me for the length of a few breaths, as though he was trying to figure me out. He looked away for the smallest of moments, then turned right back to me, almost like my necklace was pulling him. "Did you find it? Or trade someone for it?"

I peeked down at it. "No. The chain is from my parents—it was made before the bombs. The pendant is from my birth mom. She died right after I was born. She told my parents that it was special to her, and that she wanted me to have it."

Luke gazed at the Forbidden Flats again and the dust cloud disappearing far off into the distance. He didn't say a word. Eventually, he looked at me and reached out, almost as if he was going to touch the pendant but changed his mind at the last minute and pulled his hand away. "I made that pendant for my sister on her wedding day."

I grasped the pendant. I didn't understand. It took a few minutes before the pieces clicked into place and I noticed all those familiar things about him again. His thick brown hair, his skin that looked tanned, his green eyes with little flecks of gold. Did he look familiar because he looked like me? "You're . . . my birth mom's brother?"

I looked around at the others, knowing they were close enough to hear Luke and me, hoping there would be answers on their faces. But their faces held confusion and fascination, wariness and wonder.

"I don't know. Maybe. I was away when bandits hit our town—I didn't find out until I arrived home weeks later. I never saw her again." He paused for a moment. "She was pregnant. Her baby would be about your age."

No. *No.* He couldn't be my uncle. This was too weird. Things like this didn't happen. A family member you never knew existed doesn't just show up! Maybe Luke was lying. Although I had no idea why he'd lie about something like that.

"I know it isn't the prettiest stone," Luke said. "But when I was thirteen, my sister and I—"

"Anna?" I whispered.

Luke nodded slowly, as if he hadn't truly believed I had gotten the necklace from her until he heard me say her name. "Anna and I were on a trip with our dad, camped by mountains. Anna had a thing for rocks—all rocks—and she found some conglomerate ones that she loved. She put a bunch in her pockets, even though I told her they were ugly. Later that day, we found a cave and went exploring. The cave forked and Anna worried we'd get lost, but I told her it was fine—I never got lost. Still, though, she put one of those stones at each fork in the cave to mark our way. My lantern wasn't very bright, so I didn't see a large drop-off and fell."

I put my hand over my mouth to cover a gasp. "You broke one arm and cut the other," I said, remembering the story that my mom had told me many times about my birth mom. "Anna helped you out of the pit, and if it weren't for the rocks she left behind, you wouldn't have found your way out of the cave to get help before you lost too much blood."

Luke absently brushed his fingers across a scar on his left arm. "The stones didn't seem so ugly after that."

Aaren's dad searched my face as if he was trying to figure out what I was feeling. I didn't know what he was going to find. I had no idea how I felt.

"You're my uncle?" I whispered.

Everyone looked from Luke to me and back again, but I could only stare in confusion at Luke.

Aaren's dad cleared his throat. "Your sister and her husband made it to White Rock after the bandit attack. It was a long trip in a terrible blizzard. He died as soon as he got your sister here, and she lived only long enough to give birth to Hope." He paused for a minute. "They had lived in a town right near Arris."

Luke looked at Aaren's dad with sad eyes for a bit. "Hope looks like my sister."

Mr. Grenwood nodded. "I remember Anna. She does."

There was a long pause before Luke finally said to me, "My sister and I grew up in the ruins. We'll pass by them along the way to Heaven's Reach. I can show you."

I knew almost nothing about my birth mom. My whole life, I'd had so many questions about her. And now I might get to see where she grew up? Where she lived when she was my age?

The expression on Luke's face was close to what I guessed mine looked like—dazed and unsure. And so different from the way I saw him a few minutes ago, before I knew that he was my uncle.

"Think it's safe to move on?" Cole asked.

Luke shook his head, as though he'd forgotten why we were there, and looked back toward the horizon. "Yeah. I don't think we were noticed."

We all rode in silence for a long time, my thoughts a jumbled mess that I was trying to untangle. I took a breath and let some of the tangled thoughts out. "Brock, if you didn't know anything at all about your dad before he died, would you want to be told?"

"Of course! Why wouldn't I?" He looked over his shoulder at me. "Don't you want to know about your birth mom?"

I shrugged. It surprised me that I didn't know whether I did or not. I never even thought I'd have a chance to—I thought my entire birth family had been wiped out when their town was destroyed. "I've never known much about her, so I had to make up her story myself. What if I learn more, then wish I hadn't, that I could go back to believing my own story?"

"I guess that's the risk you take."

I hoped it would be a good risk. Now I just had to work up the courage to ask Luke.

# Family

The next morning, Luke rode his horse next to mine. "Are you excited to see Glacier?"

"I am. It'll be interesting to see another town."

"Glacier isn't just 'another town.'" Luke twisted in his saddle and fumbled around in one of his saddlebags. Then he pulled out something that looked similar to a tree branch or root, but made of stone. It was as long as his hand and as skinny as his thumb. It had a slightly bumpy texture with a golden color, and as he turned it, I could tell that it was mostly hollow.

"Is that"—Aaren squinted at the rock—"fulgurite?"

Luke looked at Aaren. "I'm impressed you knew that."

"Aaren reads a lot," I said.

"What's fulgurite?" Brock asked.

Luke motioned to Aaren with a flourish, so Aaren explained. "When lightning strikes sand, it super-heats it, melts the sand, and forms a rock the shape of the path the lightning took."

Luke bounced the rock in his hand once, then put it back in his saddlebag. "That's right. But do you know what was infinitely stronger, hotter, bigger, and more powerful than lightning?"

Everything suddenly fell into place. "The green bombs."

"Yep. There's a lot of places with sand around here, which means there's fulgurite buried all over this area. And not only small pieces like the ones lightning makes. Some are massive."

Aaren cocked his head to the side. "And Glacier . . . ?"

"Before the bombs," Luke said, "the place where Glacier now sits was a mine where they extracted pure silica sand." He said each of the last three words as if they had more meaning than the others.

I looked back and forth between Aaren, who stared at Luke with wide eyes and his mouth dropped open, and Luke, smiling at Aaren. "What?" I asked.

Aaren shook his head and fumbled over his words.

"That much heat, that much pressure—with silica sand, it would make glass!"

"And that," Luke said, "is how the city of Glacier was formed."

"The city walls are made of glass?" Brock asked.

"Most of them. A few months after the bombs first hit, when the weather still hadn't calmed down, bad windstorms blew through here, uncovering the top and most of the outside of it. A group of people claimed it, stuck together, and undertook the monumental job of digging out the sand from the inside, then formed a town. It's more impressive than the pyramids from way back when, if you ask me. Hopefully, one day you'll get to spend some time there when your town isn't in danger and speed isn't an issue."

As we rode toward Glacier, I kept sneaking glances at Luke, a million questions filling my mind. One of them was whether or not I could ask him a million questions, and I suddenly realized that I was ready to hear about my birth mom. I took a deep breath and then let out the question that had been burning in my mind for more years than I could remember. "What was Anna like?"

Luke smiled, as though he was glad that I asked, and I let a warmth settle over me. "Anna. She was . . . cautious.

But brave. Smart. And selfless. Extremely logical, but still easy to talk into things."

He looked up at the sky for a minute, then laughed. "Our dad—your grandpa—was a fixer. He couldn't see something broken and not find a way to fix it. He traveled a lot to scavenge things from towns with ruins. You know that since the bombs, metals can no longer hold a magnetic charge, and to make an electric motor, we need a metal that can, right?"

"Of course," Aaren said. "We learned about that back in Sixes and Sevens."

"Good. Anyway, our mom died from Shadel's when I was five, so when our dad left to go on a scavenging trip, we usually stayed in town with a neighbor lady." Luke squinted at me. "You're what? About twelve?" I nodded. "This one time," he continued, "when Anna was your age, and I was ten, our dad heard rumors of a clean zone. Kind of like the legendary Lost City of Gold, only it was our lost city of metal—a triangle of land that got missed by the overlapping circles of destruction made by three bombs. That happened almost nowhere, and he was convinced that if he went there, he could find some metals that were untouched by the side effects—that there'd be some that could hold a long-term magnetic charge. If he could find that, he could build an engine.

And he decided that it was high time Anna and I went on a trip with him.

"So we took three horses, and sped across the Forbidden Flats for nearly two weeks before we reached the clean zone."

Aaren's eyes grew wide. "It was really there?"

"Yep. A little section of land that was once called Carrington, North Dakota, including the county medical center, a dozen homes, and an office building. Completely abandoned. The office building seemed smack in the middle of the clean zone, so my dad thought it'd be our best chance of finding metals. Anna and I thought the medical center would be better—there were probably trays and equipment made of metal. It was at the very edge of the clean zone, though, so my dad didn't agree. We waited until he was busy in the office building, and we went two streets down to the medical center.

"The inside had long been stripped of any medical supplies, but it still had a few metal carts and rolling beds. The carts were thin metal, though. Anna worried they wouldn't hold a magnetic charge, so we kept looking. Finally, we found a room with a giant metal swinging arm attached to the ceiling. It was perfect. Anna thought we should run to tell our dad, but I could see how it attached to the ceiling, and convinced her we could get it ourselves."

He paused a minute and laughed some more. "Anna didn't think it would be safe, but I ignored her and started stacking things so I could climb up to reach it. I got to the top and used a rusty scalpel I'd found to turn the screws that held the arm to the ceiling. It was stuck, and when I pushed extra hard, the stack of boxes and crates and carts under me wobbled, and I lost my balance. I grabbed the metal arm and held on, and Anna dashed to the next room to get a rolling bed.

"We didn't realize the building was within the range of the bomb effects, though, and before she got back, I heard metal creak, and the whole wall and ceiling collapsed! I got knocked unconscious when I fell to the ground.

"I came to not long after. I was lying on the rolling hospital bed, and Anna was running down the streets pushing me, yelling for my dad. I felt something hard at my side, and looked over to see the metal arm on the bed with me."

We all laughed, but no one as much as me. I couldn't believe how much Anna was like Aaren, and how much Luke was like me. My mom and dad weren't daring—at least not in physical ways. Maybe my daring was something I inherited from my birth family. I had always wondered.

Luke wiped a tear from all the laughing, and I grinned.

He looked at me for a moment, then said, "You have her smile."

I looked away so he wouldn't see that my eyes watered. I had my birth mom's smile! I smiled again, to see how it felt now that I knew.

Everyone chatted as we rode, and the wind picked up. It blew in our faces for hours and hours and I didn't think it would ever stop. The wind finally died down about the time we dismounted for the day. Cole put together sandwiches while everyone watered the horses, set up their pen, and built a fire. So much dirt had hit us, I used the time before dinner to go to the horse pen and brush Ruben's coat.

When I finished, I pushed my hair off my forehead and wondered how it was possible for so much dirt to be in one place! I tried to run my fingers through my hair, but I could barely wiggle them in. And my scalp felt caked in dust. So were my skin and my clothes. And my shoes. And my bag. The wind had brought cooler weather, but that didn't stop most of us from walking right out into the river to wash off.

We huddled around the campfire, trying to dry off and warm up, before burrowing into our bedrolls. The third night in a row with no tents. It would've been nicer to have them, but everyone was tired. We all just scrunched in closer to the fire.

Aaren whispered to Brock and me, "My dad talked nonstop about Glacier City today."

"What's it like?" Brock asked.

Aaren shrugged. "He's never been there. It's right in the middle of the Forbidden Flats, and it's the only trading town in any direction for at least one hundred miles, so they have a lot more stuff than feed for the horses."

While everyone around us slept, we stayed awake, whispering about Glacier. Eventually, Brock and Aaren fell asleep, too, but I couldn't. Instead, I stared at the stars, trying to imagine how high up the Bomb's Breath was. I'd imagined the same thing inside White Rock plenty of times, but there, the Bomb's Breath touched the mountains all the way around in a circle. It was baffling to think that here, it went on and on, spreading across the immense sky in every direction.

But at least out here, it was staying the right height in the sky.

I held my necklace and brushed my finger and thumb down the smooth chain, over and over as I listened to the murmur of the river and the chirping of crickets, and thought about home and how a single necklace helped me find out I had an uncle.

# The Glass City

Luke steered his horse toward me as we rode. "Notice anything yet?"

I squinted and in the distance, I saw something shining—almost like heat waves coming off hot sand. The more I looked at it, the more I could tell that it had distinct edges, even though we were still too far away to see it well.

"Is that it?" Brock asked.

"Yes. Keep watching."

Over the next hour, the city seemed to grow bigger and bigger the closer we got to it. The ground gradually sloped down as we rode, and eventually we neared it.

After seeing it as only ripples on the horizon, I never imagined it would be this big. The gate was huge—probably twenty feet wide and twenty feet tall. It didn't look as if they broke the glass to make room for the gate. It looked like there wasn't any glass where it was to begin with. The glass started at the bottom edges of each side of the gate, and rose higher and higher as it circled around on both sides. In the parts closest to the gate where the glass wasn't very high, they built a wooden wall so that the entire city had at least a twenty-foot-high border.

When Luke said the walls were made of glass, I had thought of the kind of glass we had in windows in White Rock—mostly smooth, thin, flat, and rectangular. This was nothing like that at all. The glass was thick and anything but flat. It curved around and bent in ripples and bulges. In some places, it looked as though it might only be a foot thick, but in others, it was three or four feet thick. I could see that there were things inside the city—like houses and people—but everything was so distorted through the glass, it was impossible to tell what they were.

"This place doesn't look too friendly," Aaren's dad said.

I followed his gaze to the armed guards that patrolled the top of the city wall.

"Of course it doesn't," Luke said. "People come from all around to set up shops or to make trades. Between the goods that are held here until they're traded, and the fact that there's no one else to rob anywhere nearby, things are a little more dangerous for them. They protect themselves well."

"The walls are so tall," I said. "This whole place really used to be filled with sand?"

Luke nodded. "People can do some pretty amazing things when they work together."

We stopped our horses right before we reached the gate. Two guards stood at the top of the tall wall on either side. "State your business," one called down.

Mr. Williams slid off the trailer's bench and landed on the ground, grabbed the reins from the two horses, and walked them forward. "We're here from White Rock. We're stopping to buy feed for our horses on our way to Heaven's Reach."

The guard motioned to someone behind the gate, and after a minute, one side of the gate opened, and two more guards stood just inside it. The closest one, a burly man with short hair, spoke. "We have a strict 'no guns' policy." He motioned to the guard standing next to him, who held a big wooden box. "We'll return them when you leave. Stay on the main roads, don't start any fights, and don't cause trouble, or you'll be banned."

"We won't," Mr. Williams said to the man, then turned

to our group. "You heard him—give him your gun as you enter." He took off his gun and holster, placed them into the box, then tipped his head to the guard and rode in.

Brock and I steered Ruben as close to the glass wall as possible while we rode in. The surface in places was as smooth as the glass back home, but in other places, it was grainy—as if sand was stuck in it. On one whole section to our right, there appeared to be more sand than glass. I wanted to jump off my horse and run forward to touch it.

Brock gasped next to me, then pointed at a thick part of the wall that had something in it. "Look!"

It took a minute to figure out what I was seeing. Something big and dark was encased in the glass itself, similar to a stick in the river getting frozen in the ice during winter. "It's the scoop part of one of those tractors they had before the bombs!"

"And over there—a metal wheel!" Aaren said, pointing to another part of the glass wall. "Like the ones cars used to have."

"Stay with us," Mr. Williams called back, and we galloped to catch up with the group.

From what I could tell, Glacier City was more or less circle-shaped. The glass was shortest in the front part where we came in, and highest in the back. It was probably thirty feet high there, and curved inward, so it made a bit of a roof over the back part. A tall wooden wall divided the front half of the city from the back half. There was a road to our left, bordered with buildings. A man with a navy vest stood in the middle of the road, directing us to continue on the road in front of us.

We rode ahead to catch up with Luke, our horses' hooves clomping on the packed sand.

"What's down there?" Brock asked as he pointed toward the road the guard blocked.

"Work areas for their town," Luke said. "That entire road is off-limits to visitors. These shops," he said as he gestured to tables under wooden roofs on either side of the road we traveled on, "are run by people who come here to make trades." He jerked his head toward a shopkeeper sitting next to a table covered with a bluish cloth. The man's yellow teeth showed between his wiry mustache and beard as he called out to us about some jewelry he had for sale. "None of these people live here, except maybe in the hotel. But when the road turns left up there, you'll see the shops run by the people of Glacier. That's where the feed store is."

I tried to see everything, but there was so much, and the voices from the shopkeepers all mixed together. There were relics from before the bombs, metal bent into strange shapes, clothing, different-colored liquids that came in little jars, and trinkets that were intricate enough they must've been from before the bombs. I wished I wasn't on a horse so I could look more closely.

We rounded the corner onto a long, wide road lined with shops. Real shops. There were some that were the same as the merchant shops we had in White Rock, and some I'd never seen before. A metal shop, a tailor, one where they sold food supplies, a doctor's clinic, and the hotel. I'd heard that word before, but if Luke hadn't said it, I probably wouldn't have remembered what it meant. And they had a restaurant! I knew it was a place where strangers went to eat meals together, but I hadn't ever seen one.

People walked from shop to shop while the owners stood outside, shouting out sales or holding up items. About every five shops on each side of the road stood a Glacier guard wearing a gun in a holster on his hip and dressed in dark blue, similar to the one we saw blocking the other road. The guards scanned the crowds and the buildings, making sure there wasn't trouble anywhere.

We took our horses and trailer to a corral at the end of the street. A kid who was probably fourteen or fifteen scurried toward us and opened the gate to the corral.

On one side of the street, the backs of the buildings were against the tall wooden wall that split the circle of the city in half. Now that we were at the end by the corral, I noticed that there was a door in the wall, with two guards standing on either side.

"What's on the other side of the wall?" I asked Luke.

"That's where the people live. They have gardens along the back part—that glass overhead works like a green-house. Lengthens their growing season."

When we finished tying up our horses, Mr. Williams called out, "Mr. Grenwood has agreed to stay with the horses and trailer while I trade for supplies. Everyone else, meet back here in an hour."

"What do you want to see?" I asked Brock and Aaren. "I want to go to the bakery. And the hotel. And the restaurant."

"The clinic, too," Aaren said.

Brock, Aaren, and I started toward the buildings when Aaren's dad stopped us. "I don't want you three going off on your own. This is a dangerous place." He glanced down the street, as if there were hidden attackers everywhere, but all I saw were Glacier guards, making sure everyone was protected.

"I agree," Mr. Williams said. "I'm going to get the feed for the horses. Why don't you come with me?"

Luke slung his bag over his shoulder. "Oh, come on. They're not five. They're older than you give them credit for."

I gave Luke a look that was a million times nicer than the look Mr. Williams gave him.

"I told Hope's parents I would watch out for them," Mr. Williams said, "and I don't think they'd be too happy if I let them go off on their own in a place like this."

Luke raised an eyebrow. "They went off on their own and saved your town, right?" We did! I kind of loved Luke a little for mentioning it. "And they won't have fun in the feed store. I'll look after them."

Mr. Williams ground his teeth, and Aaren's dad squinted down the road, then gave a single nod.

"We'll stay safe," I promised. "You can trust us."

Mr. Williams looked at Aaren's dad, then said, "Okay." We took off into the town with Luke before they could change their minds.

# Exploring

We walked with Luke down the road and went inside a building with a sign that read EVERYTHING.

"This is one of my favorites," Luke said. "I think you'll enjoy it."

I didn't know where to look first. Shelves lined the walls, and tables filled almost the entire floor, leaving only small aisles to walk through. Some tables held inventions, some games, some wooden boxes of different sizes. Furniture pieces sat in a row against one of the walls. I walked over to the shelves and touched some folded squares of the softest fabric I had ever felt. I didn't know what it was made of, but it definitely wasn't the wool or cotton we had in White Rock.

Luke chatted with the person manning the shop, while Aaren, Brock, and I went to the table holding games. I felt the smooth wood of a thick, flat circle, with a ring of dips carved around the edge. Each dip held three shiny rocks. Aaren and Brock both played with a shallow wooden box that had a maze made of thin wood pieces inside it and a glass cover. They tipped the box to lead an almost perfectly round rock through the maze. I wasn't paying attention to Luke until I heard his voice perk up.

"Carl has metals?"

"Yeah," the shopkeeper said. "He traded with someone from the north a couple of days ago for a bunch of . . . iron, I think."

"Do you know where the iron was found?"

The man scratched at his neck. "I'm pretty sure it was right above Lake Superior."

"Where is Carl?" Luke asked.

He shrugged. "He was in here a bit ago, but he probably headed to his workshop. He'll be back by sundown if you want to check then."

Luke thanked the man, and steered us out of the building. Once we were on the walk in front, Luke started pacing. "There weren't bombs anywhere near that area. It may be a clean zone. I've never seen iron from there for trade *anywhere*—this could be very important. This could be it. But we aren't going to be here at sundown." Then he shook his head a few times. "I've been watching for iron from that area for years. We have to talk with him. I have to find him and see if he'll make a trade." He stopped pacing and stared toward the building, as though he was trying to see beyond it. "Carl's workshop will be on that first road we passed. It runs parallel with this road. We need to get there."

"But we can't, right?" I said. "It's off-limits. There was a guard."

"We'll have to sneak."

Aaren cocked his head to the side. "That's against the rules."

Luke started walking down the street toward the corral. "It's fine. I've talked with Carl enough that he'll understand. What's a little rule in comparison to maybe finding the metal we need to bring back electricity?"

I wasn't sure if it was bad to go, or if it was bad to turn down a possibly important discovery. Luke seemed to sense my uncertainty and said, "If you don't want to go with me, you can always go to the feed store and find Mr. Williams."

Suddenly, it felt much more like an exciting discovery than something wrong. I looked to Brock and Aaren, and it was clear they felt the same way. Besides, we were following Luke, who was an adult, and he said it was okay. "But how are we going to get to the other road?" I asked.

"The corrals. Just act normal."

Luke walked confidently down the street, and Brock, Aaren, and I did our best to look the same. When we got to the end of the shops, we were mostly hidden by our trailer, but I could still see Aaren's dad by the horses, looking bored, with the boy who helped us not far away. After a few minutes, one of the horses in the stables reared, and they both turned their attention to the horse. We used the opportunity to run to the small space between the last building and the beginning of the stables, where a water trough blocked an alley leading to the other road.

We shuffled sideways beside the trough. I lost my balance and almost fell into the water, but caught myself without making too much sound. As soon as we were past the trough, we crept the rest of the way through the alley.

Luke looked down the road at the buildings. "That one." He pointed to a building with double doors that swung open, letting in the cool air. We walked down the street and into the building, trying to look like we belonged there.

The inside looked much the same as our inventions classroom back in White Rock. There was machinery and tools for working with metal, wood, and glass, and plenty of workbenches, but there was also a large fireplace at the back of the room, with a big metal pot next to it. There were no people in sight.

"Carl?" Luke called out, not loudly enough that anyone outside of the workshop would've heard. He walked over to a workbench that held a large hammer, a couple of chisels, and two large, dark gray chunks of iron that hadn't been formed into anything yet, so they just looked like rocks. One was bigger than the other, but both were about the size of misshapen flat cantaloupes.

"Carl?" Luke said once more, his voice sounding completely distracted by the metal in front of him. He put his hands under the smaller rock and hefted it onto its side so he could see the bottom of it.

"Is it what you were looking for?" I asked.

Brock, Aaren, and I gathered around the workbench, staring at the rock, trying to guess if anything looked different from other hunks of metal.

He tilted his head and squinted. "I can't tell without doing tests. It may be. I've wanted metal from that area for more years than I can remember." His voice sounded far away. He picked up the hammer and a chisel from the workbench.

"What are you doing?" Aaren asked, alarmed.

"Carl's not here, and we'll be leaving in a few minutes.

I just need a small piece so I can test it. If it holds a magnetic charge, I'll stop by later to offer a trade."

"Hey! You shouldn't be in here!"

We all spun around to see a man—Carl, probably—who'd walked in through the open double doors, his dirty forehead crinkled in anger, his shoulders tensed, and his muscled arms crossed against a shirt streaked with coal.

"I know," Luke said. "But I heard you had this. I came to offer a trade."

"And you know better than anyone that if I had any metal for trade, it would be in the shops." Carl kept his body facing us, but looked toward the open doors. "Guards!"

"Wait," Luke said. "I know you're every bit as passionate about metal as I am. Help me out?"

The man stared at Luke for a moment, and I was sure he'd relax his muscles and his breathing. But then he noticed the chisel and hammer that were still in Luke's hands, and his eyes narrowed as three guards rushed in.

Carl flicked his hand toward us. "These four snuck in here without permission. Will you please show them the exit and let the guards at the gate know that they are banned?"

Luke struggled as two navy-vested guards grabbed his arms. "Wait! I just wanted to talk!"

Carl walked right past Luke and stopped at his workbench, his back to us. I could tell how protective he was of the metal by the way he stood between Luke and it, and that he wasn't going to talk to Luke anymore.

Luke could tell, too. He stopped struggling with the guards and walked toward the double doors leading to the street. "Come on, kids."

I ran alongside the guards. "Wait—where are you taking us?"

The guard nearest me tipped his head in the direction of the front gate. "Out of the city."

"But we're here with a group," I said. "They don't even know where we are! Can't you take us back to them instead?"

"If you don't follow the rules, you're banned." Then he ushered us to the front gate and sent us outside.

Waiting against the outside of the glass walls was awful. None of us spoke—we kept our heads down, kicking at the packed sand we stood on. From Luke's frustrated pacing, I guessed that his mind was back on the metal, and he was mad that he lost a chance at something that could have been what he was looking for.

I looked through the thick glass to see if any of the distorted blobs could be our trailer, and wondered if the others realized yet that we got kicked out. I had thought it was good to take risks. Then my mind went to the horse racing. Maybe not every risk was a good one.

After what seemed like an eternity, the gate opened wide, and Cole, Cass, Aaren's dad, and Mr. Williams rode out, leading our horses behind them. Mr. Williams walked Luke's horse and the one Brock and I shared over to us, his face furious. Luke didn't give Mr. Williams a chance to say anything—he just took hold of the reins of his horse, climbed on, and galloped ahead of everyone.

Mr. Williams watched him for a moment, then faced us. "You asked me to trust you."

"Luke told us it was okay," Brock said.

Mr. Williams looked at Brock, then the rest of us. "Did you know that road was off-limits?"

We all said yes.

"Did Luke force you to go with him?"

We shook our heads.

Mr. Williams looked right at me. "I can't trust you if you give me reasons not to." Then he turned and mounted his horse.

# Fierce Skies

The next three days tumbled together. We rode from the moment we packed up camp until lunchtime, when we ate and ran footraces against each other to make sure our legs still worked. Then we climbed back on our horses and rode until we were so exhausted and it was so dark that we couldn't make it another inch. We'd hobble around, sore from riding, to set up the tents and collapse into our bedrolls. We'd wake up and do it all over, even though I was pretty sure that none of us wanted to ride ever again.

The farther we got from White Rock, the tenser everyone got. I could see it in the way Mr. Williams and Aaren's dad rubbed their faces and fidgeted with their reins, and I could hear it in the way they spoke in clipped sentences with strained voices. Luke said that we were on the safest stretch of trail there was, but really, it wasn't the fear of bandits that was making everyone so worried. We were traveling closer and closer to our goal—finding the seforium. At the same time, though, we were getting farther and farther from home, and it felt . . . wrong. Even though I knew it wasn't.

The tensest person, though, was Cass. It was clear that she was worried about how hard we were pushing the horses, yet equally worried about not getting there quickly enough.

After we set up tents and ate dinner, we sat around the campfire to warm ourselves before crawling into bed. Mr. Williams stood up. "It's been eight days, and we haven't reached the halfway point yet. If we continue at this speed, we'll never get back in time, and I think you all know that's not an option. We need to stay on the lookout for any opportunity to make it work. To find faster ways. This was a hard decision, but I think we're going to have to leave the trailer behind and hope that when we get to Heaven's Reach, we'll be able to trade for a new one."

Mouths dropped, people sat up straighter, and we all looked at each other. No trailer?

"We won't be able to take tents, or much in the way of extra clothes, because the space in our saddlebags will have to be used for food. We'll have to find places for the horses to graze at night. We'll have to leave behind cooking supplies and tie our bedrolls to our saddles. It'll make things tougher for us, certainly. But we'll be able to ride a lot faster, and right now, that's all that matters."

Everyone was quiet after that. If they were like me, they were probably feeling a mix of worry about leaving so much of the stuff we needed behind, and relief that we could go faster, and that meeting the deadline was less impossible.

We all climbed into our bedrolls and went to sleep under tent canvas for the last time this trip.

As we warmed our freezing bodies around the campfire and ate hot granola cereal the next morning, Mr. Williams stood up to make an announcement. "Anyone tired of the scenery yet?" Most of us couldn't even manage to give him a halfhearted chuckle. Yeah, you could say we were tired of it. "Because Luke informed me that we are going to reach the ruins by this afternoon."

I sat up straight. "Really?" That was where my birth mom grew up. I would get to walk in some of the same places she walked.

Mr. Williams nodded, and the feeling in the group suddenly changed, as though someone had poured extra energy and excitement on us, washing away all the gloomy tiredness. We packed up camp in record time, stashed the trailer in the woods, and hid it as well as we could, hoping that someday we'd be able to come back for it. Then we set out for the day, each of us on our own horse now that they didn't have to pull the trailer.

"Are there homes in the ruins?" I asked as we rode.

"No," Luke said. "Not this close to a bomb. The smaller buildings were completely wiped out. The ruins are made entirely of structures big enough to not be deci-mated. The ones tall enough to use steel framework. Of course, since the bombs changed the properties of metal, the steel is no longer strong. The buildings have bent in on themselves."

"And people live there?" I asked. "*You* used to live there? Isn't it dangerous?"

"Incredibly. Everyone adapted to the weaknesses of the buildings. We learned that if we guarded ourselves well and stayed hidden, bandits weren't an issue. Each town finds their own way of making the best out of what they have, even if what they have could be perilous."

I guessed that was right. It's what we did in White Rock. Made the best of what we had, even though living that close to the Bomb's Breath was dangerous.

Lunch was the most relaxed meal we'd had in a while.

I almost didn't mind climbing back onto Ruben when it was time to leave. Almost.

The ruins were only an hour's ride farther. Luke, Brock, Aaren, and I hung back from the others so Luke could tell us story after story about his adventures growing up there. My guts hurt from laughing so much at all the ways he managed to get himself into trouble.

"You enjoyed living in the ruins," I said.

Luke gave one quick nod, then turned away.

"So why did you leave?"

A dark look crossed his face. "Because they wanted us to. We got kicked out."

"What?" I said, a little louder than I meant to. "Why would they kick you out?" My mind immediately went to the times we'd gotten into trouble on this trip—when Luke suggested we race the horses, and when Luke took us to the off-limits part of town.

"Because some of the leaders are unfair little—" Luke stopped himself, and looked to the horizon.

Dark gray clouds were dashing across the sky toward us.

"Storm coming!" Luke called out as he raced to the front of the group and pulled his horse to a stop. Everyone else steered their horses in close to him. "Storms out here approach quickly since there aren't any mountains to stop them, and spring storms are especially bad. Those clouds are bound to bring lightning—we can't be the highest thing on the Forbidden Flats, or we'll get struck. Follow me!"

As if the storm was trying to prove that Luke was correct, a lightning bolt zapped the ground in the distance, the rumbling crack of thunder catching up to us a few seconds later. We heeled our horses into a gallop and followed Luke. The drop-off between where we rode and the river was so steep, we had to ride nearly half a mile before we found a spot where we could take the horses down to the shore.

When we got to the river, we rode along the narrow shore until we reached a spot where the wall of dirt leading up to where we usually rode was higher than our heads, and we scooted in as close to it as we could.

We all pulled jackets out of our saddlebags and buttoned them to the top as the lightning storm got closer and closer. I shielded my eyes against the few raindrops that found their way to the ground, and watched. In White Rock, there wasn't so much sky to see, so we usually only saw one bolt of lightning at a time. Out here, though, lightning struck all around us, the sharp bolts spreading into a wide swath of light when they hit the air of the Bomb's Breath, then forming back into their normal sharpness as they exited the Breath and struck the ground. More than once, so many lightning bolts went through the Bomb's Breath at the same time that the lightning lit it up almost completely across the entire sky. It was one of the most beautiful things I had ever seen.

Most of the horses seemed to handle the storm just fine. I think Ruben even enjoyed it. I rubbed his neck anyway, to make sure he stayed calm. The thought of Luke getting his family kicked out of the ruins came again, so fast and hard that it hurt. I forced it from my mind and stared up at the sky.

A giant lightning bolt cracked across the clouds, as though it was splitting them open, followed less than a second later by the loudest clap of thunder I had ever heard. The hairs on my arms stood up straight, and the air felt charged, like it could explode at any second.

Then the *tap-tap-tap* of the rain against the packed hard ground came faster and faster, until it pounded down with a roar that made it almost impossible to hear anything else. We huddled our horses closer together, but still my clothes were soaked through and I was shivering violently within seconds.

"Luke!" Mr. Williams yelled, his voice barely louder than the sound of the pelting rain. "How long will this last?"

Luke shielded his eyes with his hands and looked up. "I don't know!" he yelled back. "This one looks bad."

I looked up, too. The dark gray clouds churned in the sky, moving and mixing and roiling. I couldn't see an end to them in any direction.

I ducked my head and leaned into Ruben's neck, trying to protect my body from the downpour. Then something hit me in the shoulder. Hard. I whipped my head up to see what it was as something hit me in the leg.

"Hailstorm!" Aaren's dad called out.

The pounding of the rain changed to a pinging from the hail. Another one hit me in the leg hard enough I knew it'd leave a bruise.

"We're going to have to take our chances with the lightning!" Luke yelled over the sounds of the storm. "We need to get to shelter—hail this large is too dangerous!"

# Injured

As the hail beat down on us, we rode the horses back to the incline. The ground had been packed so hard, the rain couldn't soak in. It gathered into rivers everywhere. Water cascaded down the place we needed to climb back up, making the horses' hooves slip with every step. The adults got off their horses and tried to help us, their own feet sliding in the muddy river coming down the path.

Aaren's dad, Mr. Williams, Luke, Cass, and Cole pushed against Aaren's horse, Buck, trying to help his legs stay steady enough to make it up through the mud and rushing water. Mr. Williams stopped pushing for a moment, and ducked under the strap of the bag holding the Ameiphus and handed it to me.

Over the noise of the hail, he called, "Hope, keep this out of the rain."

I took off my jacket, put the strap across my body and over one shoulder, and put my jacket back on, buttoning it to the top. Mr. Williams threw his weight into Buck's haunches, and the horse eventually made it up the incline. Brock, Aaren, and I scrambled up the muddy slope and tried to calm Buck. The others helped Ruben and then Arabelle up the pathway. I took hold of their reins and brushed streams of rainwater off Arabelle's coat.

"Maybe you should get on Buck, Aaren," Brock said. "He looks like he's about to bolt."

Aaren's horse was sidestepping and pawing his hooves into the river of rainwater running along the ground. Aaren climbed up into his saddle and tried to keep him steady. The hail was pelting into us so hard, I could barely keep Arabelle from bolting, too. Before long, they got Luke's horse up the incline; then they pushed and grunted to get Cole's horse up.

I heard shouts and turned. Cole's horse slid on the slope as the water flooded down it, and fell to the side, pinning Cass against the edge of the ravine. I watched helplessly as the others tugged and pulled and we all screamed, but Cass didn't. I wasn't sure she could even take a breath with that much weight squeezed against her.

"Push together!" Mr. Williams yelled. "One, two, three!"

As the horse's legs fumbled, they all heaved against his haunches. Then his legs caught, and his weight shifted away from Cass. Everyone pushed with their faces scrunched and their eyes determined, and Cole's horse finally made it up the incline and away from Cass.

Cass collapsed into her dad's arms, her breathing shallow, her face pained. He bent over her, trying to protect her from the hail that beat down on everything. "Cass, look at me. Can you tell if anything is broken?"

"My shoulder."

Mr. Williams carefully shifted her to see her shoulder, and his eyes widened, then flew to the side of the ravine where she had been pinned. Several rocks jutted out, one of them sharp, right where her shoulder had been.

"There's a doctor at the ruins," Luke said.

Cole scooped Cass into his arms. "I'm taking her there now. Help me!"

Mr. Williams braced Cole, keeping him from slipping, as he carried Cass up the slope. Mr. Williams scrambled up behind him, and held Cass until he could hand her up to Cole on his horse. "We'll get the last of the horses up and be right behind you." Then he whispered to Cass, "It'll be okay."

Aaren yanked a shirt out of his saddlebag and handed it to his brother. "Press this against the wound so it'll stop bleeding."

Cole took the shirt, and galloped off in the direction we had been headed, his horse's hooves splashing in the water as he rode. Mr. Williams slid back down the slope and he, along with Luke and Aaren's dad, worked to push the remaining horses up. I watched as Cole and Cass disappeared into the storm and the trees.

The hail intensified, stinging my body as it hit. Arabelle's eyes were wild, and her reins were so wet I could barely hold on to them. I climbed into her saddle so I could calm her better.

"I can't keep him still!" Aaren yelled. His horse circled wildly, his head flicking to the side as Aaren pulled on his reins.

My shoulders, my legs, and my arms were numb from the hail, and it was only getting worse. Brock climbed in Ruben's saddle, still holding the reins to Luke's horse as Luke, Aaren's dad, and Mr. Williams helped two more horses up.

Lightning crashed through the Bomb's Breath, lighting up the sky and hitting a tree not far from where we waited. The thundering *crack* came almost instantly and was so loud, we all jumped. Aaren's horse took off running. As soon as he did, Arabelle took off, too.

I peered over my shoulder as Mr. Williams yelled "Go!" to Luke and slid down the slope to help Aaren's dad push the last horse up. They were almost done.

Brock and Luke galloped right alongside me, their horses' heads lowered, their hooves pounding through the water, hail bouncing off their backs. Lightning flashed twice in quick succession, lighting up a portion of the Bomb's Breath a blinding whitish-blue.

I watched the ground, keeping the trees that lined the narrow road in my peripheral vision. The splash each hoof made as it hit the water-covered earth made me think about how Cole's horse fell on the muddy incline. *Please don't slip, please don't slip,* I mumbled over and over to Arabelle as we galloped forward.

I had no idea how long we rode, soaking wet, pummeled by hail, under a sky that alternated between violent dark gray clouds and blinding bluish-white lightning, but eventually we caught up to Cole.

Luke yelled something, but his voice was carried away by the wind.

*Crack!*

Lightning struck one of the trees directly in front of us. The light was so bright and the sound so loud, I couldn't hear anything for a few moments after. My body tingled and it felt as though the air itself was made of lightning, and I was so disoriented by the flash I couldn't tell where I was going.

When the first large shapes with sharp corners that I thought might be buildings came into view, I called out to Luke, "Are they going to let us in?"

He looked at Cass. "They have to."

I counted the rows of windows on the closest building—eight. It was eight layers high before the bombs. It looked as if the entire thing had been made of clay, though, and someone bent it right over. The first and eighth layers both touched the ground, the middle layers making a towering arch. I figured it was the way in. I steered Arabelle to ride underneath the arch and into the city, but Luke reached out and caught hold of my arm.

"It's just as likely to fall on you as not. Or get struck by lightning."

I shivered and rode as far from it as possible.

He directed us into the city, while the hail pounded with a fury on the buildings, echoing all around us. A few buildings lay completely on their sides, and some were in various states of standing up, leaning against another building, or somewhat bent and arched similar to the first. The sides of a few remained attached, so they still resembled buildings. Others had their sides blown off by the bombs and looked more like building skeletons.

The farther we went, the closer the buildings got to each other, and the paler Cass's face grew. We steered our horses single file through the narrow alleys, grateful that the tall walls blocked some of the hail. After several turns, we came to a more open space where a building lay flat on its side, its top pressed against another building that was shorter and actually standing straight up. Luke slid off his horse, walked up to a metal panel on the side of the building, and banged hard on it five times.

I didn't know enough about metals to know what kind it was, but it must've been different from the others, because the door didn't dent in and the building didn't fall. Maybe that was why this building was standing—it was different.

We helped Cass down, and Cole sat against the building, holding her. Aaren knelt next to them, pressing the soaking-wet shirt against her wound, while Brock and I stood over her as much as we could to keep the hail from hitting her.

"It's going to be okay," Cole said as he brushed some of the hail out of her drenched hair. "We'll get you to the doctor."

"Where are Mr. Williams and Aaren's dad?" I kept watching the alley we'd ridden through, but they weren't there. "Did you see them behind us?"

Cole looked up at Aaren in alarm. "I didn't. Did you?"

"I'm not sure." Aaren bit his lip. "I thought they were behind us, but I don't know if I looked."

Luke beat on the panel again. And then we waited, watching the building for the people, and watching the alley for Mr. Williams and Aaren's dad.

"Maybe the people aren't here," Brock said.

I looked around. Similar buildings surrounded us on three sides. Maybe this wasn't the right one.

"They're here." He banged again. "This is Luke Strickland! I have an injured person with me! We need help!"

Still no one came.

# The Ruins

Luke banged and banged on the door as the hail pinged off the metal of the buildings and splashed in the water streaming across the ground. I left Cass's side so I could gather the reins for as many horses as possible. With the storm this bad and the alley so narrow, I was afraid they'd run off. I turned to reach for Ruben's reins, and noticed that a man stood in an open window twenty feet up, in the building we huddled next to, and I flinched.

Then I noticed that a girl a couple of years older than me stood in the window of another building, across the alley, not quite as high up as the first. She held a bow with an arrow nocked. A half dozen archers stood at all different heights in the buildings surrounding me.

I couldn't get any words to come out. I just pointed, and everyone spun around to look.

A man about my dad's age, who stood on a chunk of broken concrete a few feet off the ground, jumped down, water spraying as he landed. The man walked up to Luke and slapped him on the shoulder twice. "Good to see you, old friend. It's been a long time."

"Good to see you, too, Jack. I wasn't sure you heard me knock."

"I think everyone from here to Glacier heard you knock."

Luke smiled. "You got room for a bunch of soaked-to-the-bone travelers, including one injured?"

The man motioned to a small group of people standing in the alley behind him. I hadn't heard them coming, or seen where they came from. A guy with big muscles broke away from the group and walked over to us.

He bent down to pick up Cass, and Cole stopped him. "I'll carry her."

The man looked at Cole for a moment, his eyebrow raised. Then, in a deep voice, he said, "I've got her."

Cole tried to protest, but the man was huge and Cole looked exhausted, so he just stayed next to Cass, pressing the shirt into her wound as they walked toward the building.

The girl with the bow and arrow who had been standing on a ledge had found her way back down, the hail that had gathered on her hat bouncing to the ground with each step. She took the horse reins from my hand. "I'll get your horses out of the storm and fed. You go with your friends."

As much as I hated leaving the horses before I knew they were cared for, I hated leaving everyone else even more. Jack knocked on the metal, and someone from the inside slid it to the right, making an opening. We all went into the building, Brock and Aaren at my side. The sound of the hail immediately quieted, and so did my hammering heart. A boy a couple of years older than me, who I had seen up on a ledge, walked in behind me.

There were no inside walls in this building—only a large open space. I could tell where each of the upper floors used to be, but there wasn't much left of them except a few pieces sticking out from the walls here and there. The floor under our feet looked as though it was made of large thin rocks about three feet square and impossibly flat, and all exactly the same shape and size, the sides and corners of each square fitting perfectly with the sides and corners of the next one, making the floor completely smooth. There were no townspeople, no beds, no places to cook meals—nothing.

I turned to the boy behind us. "Where is everyone?"

He had a look of disbelief on his face. "Did you think we'd live right here, where anyone could walk in and find us?"

"I—" I began, but then realized that my answer was yes. Where would they live if not here?

Luke started walking across the room, and I grabbed his arm. "What about Mr. Williams and Aaren's dad?"

He glanced back at the door.

"They'll never know where we are or how to find their way in here," Aaren said, panic filling his voice.

Luke motioned toward a catwalk that bordered the second row of windows up, with a ladder leading to it. "You can see everything from there. You go with the others—I'll stay and watch for them. Maybe they rode back to where we left the trailer, so they could get more supplies."

I wasn't ready to be around Luke since he said his family was kicked out of here, so I was glad for his suggestion.

"Take them to the infirmary," Jack said to the man carrying Cass. "I'll stay with Luke."

The boy eyed us like he didn't trust us and wasn't too happy that we were inside one of their buildings. Eventually, though, he flipped his light brown hair out of his eyes and said, "I'm Thomas. This way."

Thomas directed us to a space near the left wall. He pushed a dusty rug to the side with his foot, then bent down and found a place on the flat stone that had a chunk missing. When he lifted up the thin stone, it exposed a three-foot-wide square hole below it. The hole went down about eight feet, with a ladder against one of the walls.

The muscled man climbed down, and Cole and another man lowered Cass to him. She groaned at all the jostling. Then the rest of us climbed down, too. When we got to the bottom, Thomas led us down a narrow tunnel with dirt walls, a dirt floor, and a dirt ceiling. I kept an eye on the support beams that were set in the walls every few feet.

Thomas glanced up, too. "Don't worry. We haven't had a cave-in for a long time. A month or two, at least." My eyes darted to Thomas's, and he smirked, as if he was happy he alarmed me. Maybe coming here was a mistake.

At Cass's groan, the man carrying her said, "It's safe."

The tunnel was cool and our clothes were soaked, and none of us could stop shivering. Small lanterns attached to support beams lit the way enough for us to see where the walls were, but made it almost impossible to tell how far we'd been walking.

Eventually, we came to a spot where we had to turn left or right. Instead of turning, though, Thomas scooted past everyone and put his hands on the dirt wall right in front of us, pushing it sideways. It slid as easily as the metal wall had above. "The door's not dirt," Thomas said, as though he was angry he had to give up their secrets. "It just looks like it, so if anyone finds a way into the tunnels, they won't find us."

We walked through the opening and into an area bigger than the first building we'd gone into, but not as tall. This one was filled with people. Some sat on chairs sewing, some worked with wood and saws and hammers, some chopped food at big tables, and a few little kids raced through, playing chase.

Then I noticed the walls and floor—they were all made of concrete. I'd seen concrete floors plenty of times, but never walls.

"What is this place?" Aaren asked.

Thomas brushed the hair out of his eyes and frowned at us, as if he was realizing that we weren't going to disappear and that it might be easier to answer our questions. "It was the foundation of one of the biggest buildings here. The building fell over not long after the bombs, leaving this giant hole. A couple of years later, that building," Thomas said as he pointed up, "fell on top of it, making the ceiling. Back then, the people living here dug tunnels to it, filled in some holes, and made chimneys for the cookstoves and fireplaces, then they all moved in. Before I was born, they expanded to a couple of other smaller buildings with good foundations, and moved the sleeping quarters there."

Cole, Cass, and the men were halfway across the open area, heading toward a room that was apparently the infirmary. We caught up and walked inside with them, and the muscled man laid Cass on her side on a padded table. Then he handed a blanket to Cole, who laid it over Cass's soaking-wet body.

Thomas said, "I'll go get Isha," then left the room, while the muscled man put blankets over our shoulders.

"Is Isha the doctor?" Brock asked.

The man shook his head. "There is no doctor. Isha has some herbs, though. Might keep the infection out until the storm clears and you can get her to a doctor."

All the color left Cole's face. "No doctor?" He turned to Aaren. "Help her, Aaren. You have to." His voice was pleading, begging.

Aaren hesitated. "I—I don't know if I can. Her wound is so deep."

"We don't know how long it'll be until we can leave," Cole said, his voice desperate. "Or where to find another doctor. What if she can't wait that long?"

Aaren focused on the corner of the table, as though he wasn't seeing anything.

"You can do this," I said. Then I fumbled through the

bag that hung over one of his shoulders, and pulled out his med kit. It didn't have as much stuff in it as the bag he'd carried in the trailer, but hopefully it'd be enough.

Aaren didn't move. Normally, everything about him changed when he was helping someone. He became calm, focused, and confident. But not this time.

I set the kit next to him. "Aaren," I said, "this is just like helping your mom."

"I—I never really thought how it would be to do it by myself."

"You're not by yourself," I said. "You've got us, and you know what to do. You know it so well, you've sleep-talked your way through surgeries almost every night on this trip."

He blinked a few times, then looked down at his kit. "I need to clean the wound, then stitch it closed." He lifted off the wadded shirt, and Cass sucked in a sharp breath. Aaren pulled a bottle of disinfectant out of his kit and poured some into her wound, rinsing it carefully before he cleaned the skin around it with gauze. As he worked, his movements became more Aaren-like. The same as when I'd seen him help his mom.

Aaren laid out his tools to stitch the wound closed as Thomas came back into the room with the person I assumed was Isha—a short woman with bright eyes and graying hair and hands that kept fluttering, as if she didn't know whether she should help Aaren or give him space. Thomas put a hand up, letting the woman know to wait.

Cole held Cass's hand while Aaren fixed his first injury without his mom nearby. Brock stood on one side of Aaren and I stood on the other, handing him everything as he asked for it.

When Aaren finished the last stitch and cut the thread, he exhaled and sagged against Cass's bed. Then he grinned. "I did it."

I grinned back. "You did."

Aaren was still shaking. At first, I thought it was from being in wet clothes for so long—I was shivering, too— but then Brock said, "You need to eat something," and I realized how hungry I was. Isha gave us dry clothes to change into, then took us back to the main area and got us each an apple, a chunk of cheese, and a cup of water. We leaned against a table near one of the fires, thrilled to finally be warm and dry.

"Is she going to be okay?" I whispered.

Aaren stared at the concrete floor. "I think so." Then he and Brock walked back into the infirmary.

# Jumbled

I stood next to Isha for a moment, nibbling on my cheese.

"Your necklace reminds me of someone," she said, startling me.

"My birth mom—Anna—she used to live here," I said.

The woman smiled and looked up at the bricks of the building above us that formed the ceiling. "Anna. It's been a long time since I've heard that name."

"You knew her?"

"I did. I became a substitute mom of sorts after hers died. She was a beautiful girl. Smart, too. She looked like you."

I smiled, trying to hold in all the emotion I could. She knew my birth mom!

Isha asked what we were doing in the ruins, and I told her everything about the Bomb's Breath lowering and our trip. I didn't know why. There was something about her that made me feel as though it was okay to share, and I didn't want to stop talking. As though telling all of this to her was somehow like telling it to my birth mom.

When I finished, she studied me, her blue eyes intense and perceptive. Almost as if I didn't need to tell her anything, and she'd know it all just by watching me. Then she said, "Come here. I have something of Anna's that I think you should have." She motioned toward the main door we had come through.

I looked at the infirmary door, wondering if I should leave with Isha or go back in with the others. But she had something that was once my birth mom's. How could I *not* go? I walked alongside her as we left through the door covered in dirt on the outside, and walked a slight incline up a tunnel that ran perpendicular to the one we came in through. The walls were dirt, like the others, and smelled damp. I wondered if that was normal, or if it was only because of all the rain.

Isha slid open another dirt-looking door and walked us into a room that wasn't so different from the main room. Except this room was filled with beds. They were all in a chaotic order—as though maybe they were arranged in groups for families. I stared for a minute, picturing my birth mom's bed, Luke's bed, and my grandpa's bed arranged in here in a little U shape for their family.

Isha and I walked over to a bed along the back wall, and she lifted up the edge of the blanket. "Can you do me a favor and pull out that box?"

I got on my knees and reached for a square box six inches tall and more than a foot wide, then placed it on the bed. Isha sat next to it, and I sat down, too, the box between us. She pushed some trinkets to one side so she could remove a thick book with a hard cover, along with a thin notebook.

"Did you know your birth mom was an expert on rocks?" she asked.

I nodded. "Luke told me she loved them."

"The thing about your birth mom, though, is that she didn't love rocks because they were pretty or shiny. She was a smart girl—she knew what rocks and ores and minerals were made of. She could see a rock's worth based on what was inside, and what it was capable of becoming." Isha stroked the worn cover of the book. "When she was eight, her dad—I guess that would make him your grandpa—found this book in a school that was run-down even before the bombs, and he brought it to her. This book meant everything to Anna. You never saw her without it—she carried it in a bag over her shoulder at all times, this notebook with her scribblings about what she discovered nestled right by it."

Isha leaned across the box and put the textbook and the notebook into my hands. "You should be the one to have these, not me."

I looked down at the cover of the textbook—*Geology: A Study of Rocks, Minerals, Ores, and Gems.* This had been my birth mom's most prized possession. The way Isha spoke made my birth mom feel so real, I wanted her here. By me. To be the one showing me this book and her notes.

If my birth parents hadn't died, I wouldn't have my parents. I wouldn't live in White Rock. I wouldn't have my life. And although I'd never want to give that up, I still wished so many times that she hadn't died. But in all those times I wished for her to be alive, never did I *miss her* like I did right now.

More than I had ever been, I was mad at the bandits who attacked my birth parents' town. I was mad at the snowstorm that all but killed them on their way to White Rock. And I was mad at Luke. "What did he do?" I hadn't really meant to ask, but my anger made it burst out.

"What did who do?" Isha asked.

"Luke. What did he do to get their family kicked out, so they couldn't live here anymore? Because if he hadn't done it, then they wouldn't have moved to the town that got attacked by bandits. Then maybe my birth mom would still be living here, and they wouldn't have died." I didn't even look at Isha. I just looked down at the geology book, getting angrier and angrier at Luke with each passing second.

Isha reached out and put a hand on my leg. "If she hadn't moved away, then she wouldn't have met your birth dad." The calmness in her voice surprised me enough that I met her eyes. "And he's the one who helped her find her confidence again."

"Again?" I asked. "How'd she lose it?"

Isha stood up, plucked the box off the bed, and pushed it underneath where it belonged. Then she looked at me the way I remembered my grandma looking at me when I fell and scraped up my knees as a toddler. "It wasn't Luke who got them kicked out of here. It was Anna. Now pick up your books. I think we'd better get you back to your friends."

I wanted to ask Isha what Anna had done to get them kicked out, but I could tell by the look on her face that she wasn't about to tell me. I think maybe she wanted me to hear it from Luke.

Back at the infirmary, with Brock at my side and

Aaren constantly checking on Cass, I couldn't stop flipping through the book. For an entire section, each page had the name of a rock in large print at the top, showed a picture of the rock, and had paragraphs of information about it, with a chart telling about its properties at the bottom. Anna had written notes in the margins throughout the book. The notebook was set up the same way as the textbook, listing rocks with all their information. She had even drawn pictures in the places where a photograph would've been. I wished I had weeks to read everything. To know why this was so important to her.

But I didn't have weeks. I didn't even have days or hours.

I closed the two books and placed them in the bag I carried over my shoulder that also covered the bag of Ameiphus I'd been carrying since Mr. Williams pushed it into my hands. I was going to carry this book around everywhere, like my birth mom did.

I turned to Cass. "How are you feeling?"

"Better."

I could tell. Her face wasn't nearly as pale, and the circles under her eyes weren't nearly as dark.

"She doesn't have a fever," Aaren said, "but we better give her Ameiphus to be safe."

I pulled one of the pills out of the bag and handed it

to Cass. She stared at it for a moment, then looked up. "Where's my dad? Why isn't he here yet?"

Cole reached out and squeezed her hand. "I'm sure he will be soon."

"How far did Mr. Williams say this place was from Heaven's Reach?" I asked no one in particular.

"Almost exactly halfway," Aaren answered.

I felt a stabbing pain in my stomach. "I'm going to go up and talk to Luke, okay?"

Both Brock and Aaren looked at me and leaned forward, as though they were wondering if they should offer to go with me, then seemed to understand that I wanted to go by myself. I needed the long walk down the tunnel to get my thoughts unjumbled.

# Left Behind

At the end of the tunnel, I climbed up the ladder, through the opening in the stone floor, and into the main building. High on the catwalk, I found Luke using a pair of ancient binoculars to look through one of the windows, in the direction of the road we'd traveled. I climbed the wooden rungs of the ladder.

"Hi," he said, the binoculars still at his eyes.

I knew now that it wasn't Luke's fault that they had to leave the ruins. But for some reason, the anger hadn't totally disappeared.

The view from this height was incredible. The hail had stopped, and raindrops shone as they pounded down on the metal of the buildings, working to push away the remnants of anger I felt.

When I was little, my dad made me some blocks with wood left over from the lumber mill. I would stack them up, building vast cities on our living room floor, similar to the cities I saw in our history books. When Brenna was a baby, she crawled through my blocks and knocked everything down. This city here was like that—the buildings were everywhere! None of them except the one we were in stood straight. Not a single one. And the closer I looked, the more I realized that the building skeletons outnumbered the buildings with sides. It kind of looked like artwork.

"Beautiful, isn't it?" Luke said.

I nodded. It *was* beautiful.

"Have a seat."

I sat on the catwalk and dangled my legs out the window, swinging them twenty feet above the ground, not even caring that my knees were getting soaked by the rain. This window overlooked the building that was lying on its side. What used to be the side of the building—but was now its top—was almost completely removed. Its high walls protected everything inside. Corrals, pens, coops, and stalls of every size ran along the outside walls, all filled with different kinds of animals. The parts of the roof that still remained kept the rain off them. The middle of the area was grassy, and I guessed that when it wasn't stormy, many of the animals grazed there. And I could see Arabelle! She was in a mostly dry stall, munching on some hay.

"Whenever I needed to find Anna, I always checked there first."

I jerked my head toward Luke. "Really?"

"She loved animals and loved being outside. She spent every second she could down there."

I looked back at the animal area and watched the girl who had taken Arabelle's reins from me earlier. She walked along to each of the pens, completely ignoring the rain while feeding the animals, giving them water, and petting them. I imagined my birth mom doing the same thing.

Luke searched through the binoculars for a minute or two longer, then put them down at his side and sat next to me. "We have to leave without the others," he said. "That's why you're here, right?"

I hesitated for a minute, then said yes. I knew we would have to—but I hadn't admitted it to myself until just then. It wasn't even fully in my mind when I decided to come talk to Luke. But the truth was, if we waited any longer, there was no way we would get back in time to save White

Rock. We had already used up almost nine days, and we were only halfway to Heaven's Reach.

"I think Mr. Williams wouldn't want us to wait—he'd want us to try to save White Rock." Except when we were in Glacier, he didn't even want us walking down the street without him. I actually didn't know what he'd want us to do right now.

Luke shrugged. "He'd probably have a heart attack if he knew you were even thinking about going without him." He paused a minute, then added, "But he would say that the people of White Rock don't find things impossible! They *invent* a way to make it work."

I snorted at both the way he summed up my town, and the voice he used to do it. But at the same time, he was right. We always found a way—it's what we did.

"We should go," I said. "I think it's worth the risk."

"We'll go, then." He squinted out over the city. "Storm's going strong, but eventually it'll die down. The muddy roads will slow our trip, but as far as chances go, I think this is it."

"We'd have to leave Cass here," I said. "She couldn't make the trip in her condition."

"I know."

"And Cole will want to stay with her."

"Probably so." He peeked out at the storm-darkened

sky. "You get ready. I'll talk with Jack, and get him to keep someone on watch until Aaren's dad and Mr. Williams make their way here. We'll camp at the highest point we can find tonight, and I'll get some dry wood from Jack so we can build a fire. That way when the two of them get here, Jack can send them on, telling them to watch for it."

"Thanks," I said. I stood up and went to the ladder, then stopped on the first rung down. "Is it nice to be back here?"

"Yeah. It is."

"Do you think you'll ever move back?"

He looked at me for a long moment, then looked back out over the city. "No."

While Brock and Aaren were in the main room, I told them that we needed to leave. We didn't even have to ask Cole if he was going to stay with Cass. We all knew he would never leave her all alone in a strange place while she was injured and knew no one.

"I know Isha's not a doctor," I said, "but she'll take good care of Cass."

Aaren nodded.

We packed up everything we had, which wasn't much—only the stuff we happened to be carrying in our small bags when the storm hit. Then Isha, Thomas, and the muscled man walked into the infirmary and set four canvas saddlebags on the ground.

"There's bedding and food in there," Isha said, "along with some raincoats. And that one has a tent. It won't be much against the rain, but it'll be better than nothing. And they should fit with the ones you already have on your horses."

"I . . ." I was so overwhelmed with gratitude, I didn't know what to say. So instead, I reached into my bag and pulled out the smaller bag of fifty Ameiphus doses that my dad had set aside in case of emergency, and handed it to Isha. "As a thank-you."

Isha looked down at the bag of Ameiphus and smiled, the wrinkles at the sides of her mouth making little exclamation points on her smile. Then she said, "I hope you have a safe trip. And that you find lots of answers."

"I hope so, too," I said.

# The Most Basic Law

My throat tightened at the thought of leaving Cole and Cass behind, even if it was just until both their dads arrived and they caught up to us.

"You're sure you'll be fine?" Aaren asked.

"Yes," Cole said, "I think I can handle life without my little brother for a few hours."

"Take Arabelle." Cass motioned to her bandaged shoulder. "If I can't ride her, I'd rather she be with you."

"Thanks!" I was thrilled that I'd get to ride Arabelle again.

We picked up the saddlebags and followed Thomas through the main tunnel. When we reached the entrance building, Luke was waiting for us. Thomas went over to the wall and slid open a part that I had no idea was actually a door. It led into the building lying on its side that held the animals, and Thomas motioned for us to go in. The ground was muddy, and my shoes stuck in it with every step, but at least the rain wasn't falling as hard. I walked across the open space to the horses, Luke, Aaren, and Brock somewhere behind me. Arabelle nuzzled into me, and I stroked her jaw.

We brought the horses out of their stalls and put the new saddlebags on them. Then Thomas started walking toward the door that would take us back into the main building.

"We're not going out to the alley?" Aaren asked.

"No," Thomas said. "This way's a shortcut."

The four of us led our horses across the entrance building, their hooves clacking on the stone, to a door on the opposite side of the building that led to a small, closed-in area with a tiny alley leading out of it.

Aaren walked up to the underside of a building that had fallen most of the way over, making a leaning wall behind us. Pipes of all sizes came out of the building, broken from when the building tipped. Aaren reached up and touched long, skinny cords of something in reds and greens and blues and yellows, all bunched together. "Is this electrical wiring?"

"It is," Luke said.

Aaren scooted in closer, breaking away some of the colored part that seemed to be damaged by age. "This copper inside is as skinny as string! How did they ever get it formed so small?"

"Once we find some metal untouched by the bombs," Luke said, "we'll need wiring like that. I'm telling you, the person who discovers that metal will change the world."

"You've been searching for your lost city of metal for a long time," I said. "Do you think you'll keep doing it?"

"Yep," Luke said. "I'll always be searching for it. What this world needs is people to invent, and people to discover. I can't invent like my dad could, but I can discover things."

I had never thought about that before. I wondered what other things were out there that needed to be discovered and explored. Luke said we were a lot alike. Maybe I could do something similar to what he's doing—making a difference by discovering things.

Luke pulled a pocket knife out of his saddlebag and handed it to Aaren. "You and Brock enjoy inventing, right?

You should cut off a piece and take it home. Maybe you'll use it someday."

Brock and Aaren each cut a strand of it and shoved it into their bags, grinning.

"Now let's get out of here," Luke said.

We climbed onto our horses, and Luke showed us into the alleyway, which was only big enough for two of us to ride side by side. I stayed even with Luke as we wound our way through the maze of buildings. The rain wasn't nearly as bad as it had been. Eventually, we made it past the last building and onto the road, the afternoon sun peeking through one of the storm clouds and coming down in slants.

Luke nudged his horse into a gallop, and we did the same. We were moving toward Heaven's Reach again.

After a couple of hours, the rain had slowed to a drizzle, and it became dark enough that Luke worried one of the horses might injure itself on a rock or a rut that we couldn't see, so we stopped for the night. We went to the river to get a drink and to refill our waterskins, then walked the horses across the road and up a little hill. At the top of it, a big tree had fallen enough years ago that it was dried up. We all pushed on it together, scooting it far enough out of the way that we could build the fire on the drier ground where it had been.

Then we set up our tent and sat on the fallen tree, trying to warm ourselves. With the night so dark and the fire so bright, we couldn't see the road we'd traveled on, but that didn't stop us from staring that direction anyway, hoping to see any sign of the others.

"Luke?" I said, and he looked up at me, the fire casting an orange glow on his face. "Isha told me that it was Anna who got your family kicked out of the ruins."

Aaren's and Brock's heads flicked to me, and Luke looked off to the side at something I knew he couldn't see. "Will you tell me about it?"

He stayed quiet for so long that I thought he wasn't going to. Then he sighed. "Anna didn't just collect rocks or learn about them. She studied them. Came up with theories. She was searching for answers to which metals would hold a magnetic charge even more than my dad and I were. Not only did she search with us, but she researched all the time.

"Once when she was sixteen and I was fourteen, we rode with my dad to a town about twenty-five miles south of the ruins to trade. It was a long day and things didn't go well. We took a new shortcut home. After a few miles, we spotted a dry riverbed, and Anna was convinced that she could see a new kind of stone, even while up on her horse, and she wanted to spend some time cataloging. We were irritable and exhausted and the horses were tired, and my dad said no.

"So we went home. Then, when it got dark, Anna snuck out and went to the riverbed. Right after she found the rocks, bandits found her. She raced away on her horse, and lost them."

Luke looked up from the flames for the first time, and met my eyes. "You've seen the people in the ruins. Safety's so important to them, they're willing to live underground. They have a belowground water system so they don't have to be seen. The city doesn't even have a real name, because they think that'd make it a target. They have very strict protocols to ensure their safety and protection.

"One of those protocols is, if you are being chased by bandits, you go to the building on the southernmost end, and sound the silent alarm. Help will come, and they'll prevail because they can fight back with the element of surprise, and keep the conflict away from where they live."

Luke's eyes went back to the fire, and he dropped his voice low enough that I had a hard time hearing him above the crackling of the flames. "Anna thought she'd lost the bandits, so she didn't go to the safety building—she went straight to the front door of the main building. As soon as they opened it to let her in, the bandits attacked."

We all gasped.

"What happened?" I asked.

"We fought back and won. We kept our secret safe, but a lot of lives were lost. When Anna violated the protocols for being followed by bandits, she broke the most basic law in the ruins, so she was banned. She made one stupid mistake, and they kicked her out, when I made so many—" His voice cracked, and he stopped talking.

I stared into the fire, imagining what my birth mom must have felt when she realized what she'd done.

After a minute, Luke spoke again. "Anna was convinced that she could find our lost city of metal."

"Did she?" I asked.

Luke shook his head. "When we got kicked out, she said that it was her obsession with rocks that caused all the trouble. So she left her books behind, along with any desire she had of figuring it all out. She didn't pick up a single rock or go on another exploring trip with us ever again."

Luke looked at me for a moment, then stood up and went to the tent.

I didn't move from my seat on the fallen tree. Brock and Aaren stayed with me. It made me sad to think about my birth mom's dreams and plans, and to know that she never accomplished them. I lifted the flap of my bag and pulled out the two books—the textbook and the notebook—that she'd left behind. I brushed the tips of my fingers along the words that she had written. Somewhere in these were the clues to her theories. The things that might've helped her unlock the secrets of the lost city of metal, if she hadn't quit trying.

I decided that I was going to help my birth mom finish what she no longer could.

# Negotiator

I knew that the sun was about to poke the first bit of its head above the trees in the east, because it finally got light enough that I didn't have to squint so much to see the words of Anna's book. That meant my time had run out. We needed to be on the horses every second that the sun was up, or we'd have no chance of making it back to White Rock in time.

Luke ducked under the tent flap and stepped out into the clearing near the ashes of last night's fire. He glanced at me, then to the road, a strange expression on his face.

"What?" I said.

He paused, then ran his hand through his hair. "Nothing. You just looked like Anna for a minute. No sign of Mr. Williams or Aaren's dad?"

I spun on the tree trunk toward the road. I had been so focused on the book that I hadn't even thought of them!

"They haven't come?" Aaren asked as he and Brock climbed out of the tent.

"No," Luke said.

Aaren walked a few paces to get a better view of the road. "If they made it to the ruins, they would've ridden all during the night to get to us. They'd be here."

"Something must've held them up." Luke took one last look at the road. "And we've got no time to wait. That means we're on our own from here on out."

I gulped and tried to see the look on Aaren's face. But he started packing up camp, so the rest of us did, too.

As we folded up the tent, Brock said, "You're okay with leading the negotiations now that Mr. Williams won't be there to do it, right?"

"What?" I practically yelled. "Me?"

Luke gave me a half-smile. "I guess you hadn't thought that far yet, huh?" He put his hand on my shoulder. "Of course it's you. I don't have the authority. Your dad is the council head—the mayor of Heaven's Reach probably won't talk to anyone but you."

"But . . . I don't have any idea how to do something like that!"

"You'll do fine," Aaren said.

I was pretty sure I wouldn't!

"We'd better go," Brock said. "We can enjoy that freaked-out look on Hope's face along the way."

After a few minutes, Luke rode right beside me. "You're brave. Why are you so nervous?"

I frowned. "I'm bad at that stuff. I can't talk adults into anything."

"I heard you saved your town before. I bet you didn't think you could do that until you did."

"Only because I found a way to use my strengths. But my strengths aren't exactly the kinds of things that help in most situations. How often do people need someone to sky jump off a cliff?"

He held up his hands in surrender. "The way I see it, you've got some pretty valuable strengths."

"And some pretty impressive weaknesses," I said. "This is one of them. When I said I'd come on this trip, I didn't think I'd have to do anything like that. If I fail, we lose our town."

Luke stayed quiet for a long time before he spoke again. "My dad—your grandpa—always said, 'Sometimes you won't have the tools you need. But just because you don't have a wrench doesn't mean you can't use needle-nose pliers to do the same job.' "

"So . . . ," I said, "tools are what? Your strengths?"

He nodded. "When bandits invaded, you went all the way over White Rock's crater to Browning during a terrible snowstorm, right?"

"Yeah."

"You keep going when things get bad enough that most people would stop. So that means you're persistent—that's like your hammer. You got others to follow you, so you're a good leader—that's your screwdriver. And you're brave enough to take risks that would scare other people. That's your needle-nose pliers." He grinned. "I think you got that from my side of the family, by the way."

I raised an eyebrow. "Oh, yeah?"

He looked amused. "The point is, sometimes when you need a wrench and you don't have it, needle-nose pliers will work well enough."

*Well enough.* I wasn't sure "well enough" was going to save anyone.

We rode all day until it got too dark, then led the horses to the river to drink. The river was wider here, and not all together, the way it was in most places. It was as if the river had split into five or six rivers, with a tiny section of land in between each one. It was at least one hundred feet wide, but probably not very deep—I guessed that was why nobody took boats on it. It wasn't shallow enough to cross, though.

"Is there a bridge anywhere on this river?" I asked.

Luke flicked his hand downstream. "Yeah—there's one close to Heaven's Reach, for anyone who needs to go up and around to the west side of the Rockies."

"Then why doesn't anyone live on that side?" Aaren asked. "They'd have the river protecting them from bandits."

"Wind."

I looked at him. "Really?"

"The old timers say it wasn't bad before the bombs, but it's definitely bad now." He let out a little laugh. "A couple of years ago, not long before my dad died, we had to go to Downwind—a town a little south of Heaven's Reach."

"What?" Brock exclaimed. "The town's name is Downwind?"

"Yep."

Aaren wrinkled his nose. "Who would want to go to a place like that?"

"That's exactly why they gave it that name. To keep

people away. But my dad and I had been there before, and we needed to make a trade with them. We decided to take a shortcut, and we came down that side of the river.

"For the first hundred twenty-five or so miles, everything was fine, and we hadn't come across a single bandit. We'd patted ourselves on the back for taking such a brilliant route. Then we hit the wind. It was a constant blow-you-backward sort of wind. The kind that makes you feel as though you're walking in place. We'd hoped we'd hit a storm, but it wasn't—it was a wind tunnel coming right from that gap down there between those two mountains.

"It kept blowing and blowing and blowing. So much that we couldn't set up a tent at night. We had to find a big boulder or a rise in the land to shield us from the wind. I guess there's a good reason they call it Desolation Alley. It took us eleven days to get through it, the wind blowing into our faces the entire time. Every bit of skin was as dry and cracked as the desert by the time we reached the end. Even my eyeballs." He winked at me. "My dad and I always joked that neither of us was allowed to come up with a brilliant plan ever again."

I laughed. "And did either of you?"

"Of course we did," Luke said. "We're Stricklands. We always come up with brilliant plans."

"Like your plan to find the lost city of metal?" Brock asked.

"Hey," he said. "I'll find it. It's too important not to. I'm not just talking about being able to turn on a light-bulb or power refrigerators—we could have ways to communicate across towns. Across the country. Even across the world. And when people can communicate, they can work together. When each town isn't trying to reinvent the wheel themselves, the whole world will progress again."

"How do you know it's even out there?" Aaren asked. "If you found that spot in North Dakota and there weren't any metals that were usable, what makes you think they'll be somewhere else?"

"Because they have to be. The ability to make electricity and electric motors again is what will drive civilization forward. My dad wouldn't have spent his whole life searching for it if it didn't exist. It has to be out there somewhere."

I remembered something I'd read that morning. "In her notebook, Anna wrote in the margin that when metals change, they move in the same direction. It seemed like she thought it was important."

"What does that mean?" Brock asked.

I shrugged. "I have no idea—it almost feels like some kind of riddle. I wondered if maybe it meant that the metals that were changed by the bombs were only changed in lines. Maybe like spokes on a wheel moving out from where a bomb hit."

"But that doesn't make sense," Aaren said. "They were changed everywhere, not just in some directions."

Luke chuckled. "I never understood what she was talking about when she said that. I decided years ago that she just told me it was one of her theories in order to drive me insane."

"I hope that someday you'll figure it out," I said.

Luke smiled as we led the horses back up to the road. "Me too."

# Small Discoveries

I jolted awake, my mouth tasting like horse, and wiped my drool off Arabelle's neck. I was so tired from waking up early to read Anna's books that by the time afternoon hit, I couldn't seem to keep my eyes open no matter how hard I tried.

"Have a nice nap?" Brock asked, his mouth twitching.

"I didn't laugh in my sleep again, did I?"

"No," he said. "You mostly snored into Arabelle's neck." And then he made a snoring sound while fluttering his fingers in front of his mouth, mimicking Arabelle's mane.

"Are you finding anything in her books?" Aaren asked.

I was mostly getting frustrated. I wished I'd had Aaren's science brain so I could understand all that I was reading better. I reached into my bag and pulled the text-book out. "The beginning talks about boring stuff. But here"—I opened it to the back section—"it tells about all different kinds of minerals and ores. See? Each page has a picture of one and a list of facts." Then I pulled out her notebook. "Her notes in here are set up the same, but with rocks that aren't in the textbook."

Aaren steered his horse a little closer, and leaned toward the notebook. "Maybe the rocks in the notebook are the ones that have changed since the bombs."

"I think so," I said.

Luke kept his eyes on the pathway ahead, but said, "Anna told my dad and me that she didn't think iron any-where would be able to hold a magnetic charge. That it didn't matter how far from the bombs it was, it would all be affected."

"Really?" I said. "Did you think she was right?"

"Of course we didn't! It has to be somewhere. It *has* to be."

"But she kept searching for your lost city of metal," Brock said, "even after she guessed that no iron anywhere would work?"

Luke nodded. "I still think the key is to find iron that was completely protected from the bombs. We haven't found it yet, but we will."

Maybe Luke was right. Or maybe Anna was. Only I couldn't help thinking that she was recording everything she found out about new minerals and ores because she was trying to understand what they had in common. Because maybe if she figured out what changed, she could figure out how to find magnetic metal. I looked down at the notebook in my hands, then at Aaren and Brock. "Will you help me? Maybe with all of us, we can make sense of it."

Sometime after I realized that the bumpy horizon I could occasionally see between the trees was actually the Rocky Mountains, I remembered about the negotiations with the mayor that I was now in charge of. How was I supposed to know how to negotiate? I couldn't even talk myself out of detention. And now that there were only four of us, we couldn't search for a seam of seforium to mine ourselves as a backup plan. I *had* to talk the mayor into giving it to us.

The bag of Ameiphus over my shoulder felt heavy, as though it was trying to drag me down. I put my hand on it and felt something hard. When I looked inside, I found the seforium rock among the Ameiphus pills, and held it up high, the orange hue shining in the sun.

"You okay?" Aaren asked, looking at me with a concerned face.

I put the rock back into the bag and almost said that I was fine, but at the last second, "I'm nervous" came out instead.

"About the negotiations?" he asked, and I nodded. "Remember back on your front porch, that night when we decided to come on this trip?"

"Yeah."

"We really didn't have any idea what we were getting ourselves into, did we?"

I thought back to how many things had happened on this trip that we hadn't anticipated. "No, we really didn't."

"We'll help you get ready," Aaren said. "We'll give you tips. Like . . . compliment him, but don't overcompliment because then he won't think you're sincere."

"And try to forget what's at stake so you won't be nervous," Brock said. "Don't let *him* forget what's at stake, though."

"Don't show all your cards at once or you lose negotiating power," Luke said.

"If things aren't working out," Aaren said, "start to cry; he'll get all flustered and give you anything you want."

"No, don't cry," Brock said. "Be strong—as if there's no way you're going to let him bully you."

"Ask lots of questions, so you can find out what's

important to him, and then let him think you're giving him what he wants."

"If he isn't willing to give you everything you need, walk away. Then he'll be more willing to talk it out."

"Don't tell him how much Ameiphus you have."

"Don't rush the negotiations. But remember that the Bomb's Breath is getting lower and lower every single second."

"Stop!" I yelled. All this advice was making it hard to think. I was even less sure I could do this now. I steered Arabelle a little away from the others, so my brain could quiet. It's not that I was afraid to try. But at home if I failed at something, it didn't matter much. Here if I failed, my town would lose everything. It scared me.

That night, after everyone had crawled into their bedrolls, I couldn't fall asleep. I missed my parents. I wondered how everyone in town was dealing with the fact that the Bomb's Breath was getting closer and closer. My stomach felt sick from all the layers of worry piled on top of each other—worry for Cole and Cass, worry for Mr. Williams and Aaren's dad, worry for the people back in White Rock, worry that I'd never figure out what my birth mom had been trying to figure out, and most of all, worry for the negotiations.

I sat up. There was no way I was ever going to get to sleep if I let my mind continue. And if I kept lying there, my mind was never going to stop. I pulled the smaller, softer blanket out of my bedroll, crawled out of the tent, and wrapped the blanket around my shoulders. Tonight was the warmest, clearest night we'd had in days. I sat on the roots of a large tree, leaning my back against its trunk. I didn't see that Brock had come out of the tent, too, until he sat down next to me.

"Can't sleep?" he whispered.

I shook my head, then adjusted my blanket so it covered both of our shoulders. "Do you miss your family?"

He let out a quiet laugh. "I lived in White Rock without them for almost a year. I can handle being away from them for this long."

I could tell by his voice that he did miss them, though. "They've only been in White Rock with you for a month. It's okay to miss them."

He stared into the fire. "I don't know. Maybe I shouldn't have left without telling my mom. It's just—"

I watched his face and tried to figure out what he wasn't saying.

It was a while before he spoke again. "It's important to stick together. You were there when I needed help, so

I should be here helping you—not sitting at home doing nothing."

I thought back to how I felt before I knew I could come. I wouldn't have been able to sit home and do nothing, either. "I'm glad you're here."

"So," Brock said, "how long after we get back before you leave again for weeks to go exploring?"

I laughed. I wanted to go out exploring again sometime. I did. But I knew Brock would be the first of us to miss this, and to be aching for the next adventure. "Give me a few weeks to recover from all this horse riding. Oh, and you'd better give my parents a good ten years to get over saying yes to me going on this trip."

Brock raised an eyebrow and scoffed. "As if you could wait ten years to come out here again. I've seen the way you look at all this open space. There's no way you could sit at home."

"Sure I could," I said. "I'm thinking of learning how to knit."

He chuckled, and I gazed down at my hand on my knee, suddenly very aware of the fact that we sat so close together that our knees almost touched. And then Brock moved his hand forward and linked his pinky finger in mine.

He looked up at the stars, and I looked at our pinkies. Was this because he missed his family? Or was this him showing me that he *liked*-liked me? And if he did actually like me, would that make being my friend weird? No. He didn't *like*-like me. We were just friends. Right? I couldn't figure out how to ask him without it being awkward.

Who needed the ability to communicate with people across the world? I couldn't manage to communicate with the person sitting next to me. "We'd better get to sleep," I blurted out.

He agreed, and I let go of his pinky and took my blanket back to my bedroll. Yeah. I was going to have no problem at all falling asleep now. *No problem at all.*

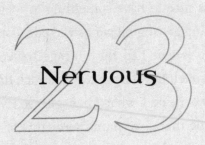

# Nervous

Trying to figure out the things Anna hadn't figured out about the metals was a great distraction. It kept the hours and hours we spent on horses from being so monotonous, and kept the anxiety for our town from making us sick. But our progress on figuring any of it out remained exactly zero. Aaren was somehow managing to read Anna's textbook and notes while riding on his bumpy horse. He blurted out that iron wasn't the only metal that could hold a magnetic charge—that there were four others that could, too. We thought we had found the solution. But then Luke said that all five could no longer hold a permanent magnetic charge. He had already checked each of them.

So we were back to square one. Every time we thought

we'd figured something out, we'd realize we hadn't figured anything out at all.

The Rocky Mountains were finally in view over the trees. It was nice to have something to focus on, and to see something getting bigger as we rode along. Especially since we no longer had the mileage trackers, so it was impossible to tell how far we traveled each day.

When we neared what Luke guessed was the four-hundred-mile mark, we found remnants of homes. They weren't complete homes—everything we saw had at least two sides missing, but there were parts there! Some had parts of kitchens in them still—cabinets that hadn't been completely destroyed, sinks, refrigerators—and a few houses even had a bathtub or toilet, all covered in years of dust and dirt and leaves that had blown in. I imagined the family who might've lived in each one.

That afternoon, Luke informed us that if we rode hard, we would get to Heaven's Reach by tomorrow, and Aaren, Brock, and I cheered. If we arrived tomorrow, then that meant we'd made the last half of the trip there in just four days.

"Luke," I said, "what are the people of Heaven's Reach like?" I figured it was better to know. Sometimes my brain thought of the worst when it was left to wonder.

Luke shrugged. "They're open to trade, if it benefits

them. They're sitting on a wealth of minerals, and there are things they could use that they don't have. I met the mayor once—we were both in Downwind at the same time."

"What's he like?" Brock asked.

"Pompous. Thinks he's better than most people. Focus on getting him to like you, and you'll be fine."

I was going to be sick.

"You should go up there with us," I blurted out.

Luke studied me, as though he was trying to decide if I was serious. "Through the Bomb's Breath."

"I know you can do it—it's not that hard," I said. "We can show you." I paused for a minute, and Luke didn't say anything. He just sat on his horse looking unsure.

Then he said, "I can't very well have my niece besting me when it comes to being daring now, can I? Once we get there, show me."

When I woke up in the morning, I brushed Arabelle's coat before I put her saddle on. "It's okay, girl. A little farther, and you'll get to rest."

The mountains looked even bigger, and we rode into areas with deeper and deeper drop-offs. The ground would be level, then suddenly it would dip down, and after a few miles, it would rise back up.

At the second drop-off, Luke gestured toward the space. "Before the bombs changed the flow of rivers, these were lakes."

"I was wondering," Aaren said. "The soil is different here—like dried-out sediment."

The mountains that formed White Rock's crater and surrounded us back home were big. But I couldn't believe the size of the Rocky Mountains! They made White Rock's seem teeny. The closer we got, the more they towered over us, and made *me* feel teeny. Like an ant. And they kept going for as far as I could see in either direction. I had been amazed by the Forbidden Flats and how they went on forever. I think I was even more amazed by the mountains, and how they went *up* forever.

As we rode, I noticed some ruins in the distance—far off to the left of where we were headed. It was from a city that must've been much larger than the ruins Luke and my birth mom were from. There were dozens and dozens of buildings glinting in the sun, angled every direction imaginable.

I pointed to them. "Do people live there?"

"Yep," Luke said. "Several hundred, actually. That's Downwind."

"*That's* Downwind? That place looks like a death trap!"

"It is," Luke said. "At least it is to outsiders—the metal

on the buildings' framework is very unstable. The people who live there know the tricks of every spot, though, and have a nice town set up in the middle."

That made me think of the story Luke told about his dad saying you could use a different tool when you didn't have the right one. Maybe every town turned one of their weaknesses—or one of their dangers—into a strength. Into something that could protect them.

Even though the mountains looked close, it took four hours for us to get there. Luke pointed ahead to a place at the base of the mountains. "See those two ridges that form a V where the mountains rise almost straight up? That's where we're headed. There's a waterfall coming off that ridge to the left of the V. It's nice and cold from the spring runoff. We'll find a spot not far from there where we can leave the horses."

I hadn't even thought about the fact that we wouldn't be able to take the horses up to Heaven's Reach. I panicked for a moment until Luke said, "It'll be okay. I'm good at finding places to picket a horse where it'll be safe."

When we finally made it to the V in the mountain, we ate a quick lunch of stale rolls, some beef jerky, and an apple.

My hands were shaking while I tied Arabelle to a tree in the area Luke showed us. I grabbed hold of the bag of

Ameiphus over my shoulder, to make the shaking less obvious. I had never been this nervous before.

"Will you go with me?" I said to Luke. "When I talk to the mayor, can you come in with me to make sure I don't say something stupid or forget to ask something, or help me if I don't know what to say?"

Luke looked up the mountain, probably to where the Bomb's Breath was, seeming rather nervous himself. After a minute, he turned back to me and said, "Sure. You aren't going to need me, though."

I was so relieved that he said yes!

Luke took us to the base of the mountain and up a zigzagging trail full of switchbacks that led to Heaven's Reach while I thought about all the advice they had given me. I was pretty sure I couldn't do even one of those things right. Luke was wrong. I was going to need him. A lot.

The path was steeper than anything we had to climb to get to the Bomb's Breath in White Rock. A lot less dirt and a lot more rock covered the trail, too. It wound back and forth, getting close to the waterfall, then getting farther away, then back again. We waved our arms above us almost the whole way to feel for the Bomb's Breath, but we hadn't felt it yet when we reached a set of stairs carved into the stone.

"From what I know, the Bomb's Breath begins here." Luke took a few steps back down the path.

"All you have to do is hold your breath," Aaren said.

"And then feel around to see where it starts." Brock waved his arm in the air to demonstrate.

"No matter what," I told Luke, "don't breathe until you are absolutely sure that your head is out of the Bomb's Breath. Even if something startles you or if you have to stay in it longer than you planned. Not even a teeny tiny breath." When I saw the look on Luke's face, I realized that I had done the same thing everyone else did when they were giving me tips on negotiating—said way too much. "Sorry. All you really need to know is to hold your breath while you're in it."

"Ready?" Aaren asked.

Luke nodded. Aaren and Brock went ahead of us; then I put my arm up to see where the dense air began. "See? It's right here. Feel it." Luke waved his arm where I showed him, a look of fascination on his face. "Now take a breath," I said, and then we walked up the stairs.

The Bomb's Breath covered everywhere the same as it covered White Rock, and it was all the same thickness as it was back home—fifteen feet, but climbing up stairs made it seem much faster, because we were going uphill so quickly. It was strange—I was in a place I'd never been to before, but walking through the Bomb's Breath made it feel a little like home. Within moments, I felt my head break out of the dense air, and I told Luke he could breathe again while we climbed the last few stairs.

He took a breath. "That was . . . interesting." He dipped his foot back into the air of the Bomb's Breath and moved it around. "Huh."

I was proud of him. And proud of me for talking him through it.

"Can we help you?"

The voice startled me. I spun around to find two guards standing not far from us on the other side of a small clearing, in the shade of some aspen trees. One of them—a big man with a thick beard and a bald head—looked surprised to see us. The other guard was a tall, thin woman who narrowed her eyes.

I took one stride forward and made my voice sound as adult as possible. "We're here representing White Rock, and we need to talk with your mayor about a trade."

"Wait here," the man said. "I'll inform the mayor." Then he walked into the trees.

# Heaven's Reach

We waited a long time before the guard returned, and it felt even longer with the other guard staring at us the whole time. I didn't think she appreciated strangers. And based on how often she peered over her shoulder to see if the other guard was on the trail behind her, I guessed she didn't expect him to take so long, either.

When the guard finally returned, he said, "Follow me," and took us along an overgrown pathway meandering through the aspen trees. In a few minutes, we stepped out of the trees into a clearing overlooking a small valley. The guard gestured to the area in front of us. "Welcome," he said, "to Heaven's Reach."

We were on a hill only about ten feet higher than the

valley, and a hundred yards from the nearest building, but from our vantage point, we could see all of it. The ground the city was on was mostly flat, but sloped slightly uphill as it went back; then the mountain rose straight up behind it. The mountains curved, and the layout of the town curved, too. Almost as if a giant had scooped the area for the town right out of the mountain itself.

The building closest to us was large and bent the opposite direction of the mountain. Then there was a grassy area, and three rows of homes curved the same direction as the mountain right behind it, as though they were all forming a giant piece of pie, with roads at both sides of the pie.

The most incredible part of it all was a towering sculpture that stood in front of the main building. It was made from lots of different kinds of metals, each a distinct shade, from almost whitish-silver to a dark pewter gray to metals that were slightly red, orange, brown, or blue. Some were shiny and others were dull. Each of the metals started with the others at the base, then rose outward and upward, as if they were all reaching toward the sky, some twisting as they went up. In the middle of it all was a glass ball, about the size of a watermelon, only round, and filled with an orange powder. The metal around it was almost white, so the sun caught it and made the ball look like it was glowing.

"This place is amazing!" Aaren said.

Luke raised his eyebrows. "I'm impressed. The mayor talked big about this place when I saw him, but I guess I thought he was embellishing."

We walked across the clearing toward the building with the grass in front. Hundreds of people—probably their entire town—gathered in groups on the grassy hill, finishing their lunch. Everyone stopped what they were doing to watch us. I straightened my shirt, and suddenly wished I'd thought to brush my hair before we came.

A girl stood in front of the building, on a strip of gravel that separated it from the grass, with her shoulders back and her hands clasped in front of her. Her hair fell down her back in curls and was a coppery color like no one's in White Rock. It shone in the sun. She stared at us with bright green eyes and a strange look on her face. The guard with us moved to her side.

I stood straighter, because it seemed to matter, and tried to figure out why she was looking at us that way. The guard cleared his throat. "This is Alondra. She's the daughter of the mayor. Alondra, these people are here representing White Rock."

She gave a little curtsy.

"Thank you so much for inviting us into your town," Luke said. "It's quite an honor to be here." He bowed. I didn't know what to do, so I bowed, too. The girl smiled, as if she found it funny. Did I do something wrong? "This is Hope," Luke said as he gently touched my back. "She's the daughter of Council Head Toriella in White Rock, and my niece, and she's come to talk with the mayor about a possible trade for seforium."

Maybe now was the time I was supposed to bow. I bowed again, feeling awkward. "Hi," I said. "Nice to meet you."

"And you," Alondra said.

Then Luke introduced Brock and Aaren. Aaren reached to shake Alondra's hand. I should've offered to shake hands instead!

"Your city is incredible," Aaren said.

Alondra smiled, and I beamed at Aaren. How did he always know what to say? Brock shook Alondra's hand, too, but didn't say anything.

"It's nice to meet you all. We do mine seforium here," Alondra said, and a huge weight lifted off my shoulders, "although I'm not sure we have any to trade. I regret to inform you that my father is tied up with some business away from town, and he won't be able to meet with you.

If you'd like to wait a few days, though, then you are more than welcome to."

The relief I felt vanished, and panic rose in its place.

"A few days?" Brock groaned. "We don't have a few days!"

"We don't," I said. "Isn't there any way to talk with him sooner? It's urgent. Our entire town is in danger!"

Alondra looked startled. I didn't know if it was because we had yelled or because I said our town was in danger. I tried to calm my voice, but it still came out shaky. "Please. We live inside one of the craters from a green bomb, and the Bomb's Breath over our crater is lowering. We need seforium to fix it. Everyone in my town will have to leave if we don't make it back soon, and it already took longer to get here than we had planned. If we wait for a few more days, it'll be too late. We'll have to abandon White Rock."

Alarm and sympathy showed on Alondra's face. "I'm sorry," she said. "He's in Downwind making trades. There's no way for me to contact him."

"I'll go find him," Luke said. "Let him know it's an emergency." He started running toward the woods leading to the pathway and called out, "Be back soon."

Aaren, Alondra, Brock, and I were left in uncomfortable

181

silence. I looked at Alondra, wondering if we should head back down to the horses, or if we should wait here.

"Follow me," she said, and she led us back through the clearing and into the trees. I walked straight-backed the whole time, the way she did, practicing being proper. It reminded me of when we learned about royalty in history class. I didn't think I'd see it in a town in the Rocky Mountains, though. Right before we reached the trees, she looked over her shoulder, as if she was checking to see if anyone was watching.

As soon as we had all entered the woods, she spun around. "You're kids!" Brock and Aaren and I glanced at each other, then back to her, confused. "I apologize," she said. "It's just that we've never had visitors who were kids before!"

I laughed. What happened to acting like royalty?

"And you go through the Bomb's Breath. People almost never come here—we usually make trades down below. Some get impatient and brave the Bomb's Breath to talk with my dad sooner. A few even die trying, but kids never come here!" She looked at each of us. "I'm rambling. Tell me about you."

"Um," I said, suddenly unable to think of a single thing I liked to do. "Aaren likes science and inventing, and he's practically a doctor. Brock likes a challenge."

"And Hope likes beating me in a challenge," Brock said.

Alondra's eyes lit up. "Really? Do you Sky Surf?"

"Sky Surf?" Aaren asked.

"You live in a crater with mountains, right? And you said you have the Bomb's Breath."

"We sky jump," I said. "I don't know if that's—" We all looked at her with confused faces.

"Come on," she said, and took off running through the trees.

# Sky Surfing

We stood there, watching Alondra as she ran several yards into the trees, then turned around and stopped. "Are you not coming?"

I glanced back toward the clearing, then in the direction of the pathway that would lead us back down. "I'm sorry. We really don't have time to play. Or . . . Sky Surf. Our town's in danger, and we need to get home quickly."

She walked back to where we stood. "Downwind is a good hour's ride each direction, and it'll take time for your uncle to find my dad and convince him to leave. Would you rather go down to your horses to wait? Or have me show you my town?"

"I—" What I really wanted was to do something—

anything—that would help us to make the trade and get back on the road more quickly. But there seemed to be nothing we could do yet. "I don't know." I looked to Aaren and Brock for help in figuring out what we should be doing right now.

They both shrugged.

Alondra regarded us for a minute. "Waiting will seem to take forever if you're not doing something." She turned to Aaren. "You like to invent, right? Aren't you curious to see the Sky Surfboard inventions?"

Aaren's eyes lit up. I knew he was dying to see them.

She looked back at me. "We won't be gone long. And from the cliff's edge, you can see Downwind and the entire path there. We'll be able to see them coming back."

I looked at Aaren's face filled with curiosity, and had to admit that mine probably looked the same. Brock's, too. We came from a town of inventors—we *should* try to learn from other towns' inventions. I nodded. "Okay, we'll go with you for a little while."

Alondra ran through a path that wasn't really a path, pulling her hair into a ponytail as she ran. We crashed through the trees behind her until she stopped right at the edge of a cliff by a wooden chest. She pulled out a board made of thin wood, and held it up, a question on her face. We stared at her blankly. It was probably three feet long and a foot and a half wide, with extra flap pieces sticking out on both sides. Two stick-like pieces stuck straight out of the top, and a hole was drilled in the bottom center. Alondra held the board in front of her by the handles, as if we'd realize what it was if we looked longer.

But we didn't. She pulled out a second one and handed it to me. Then she picked up two things that looked like misshapen bowls, with strings attached to either side. Next came two skinny bundles about six feet long. Each of the bundles looked as though it had a couple of pieces of wood with fabric bunched around them. We carried everything to the edge of the cliff.

I set the board on the ground when Alondra did the same; then I held up the bowl thing. "What's this?"

"It's a null." She crinkled her forehead. "You don't use a null when you sky jump?"

"Uh . . ." I looked down at the object in my hand. "No."

Alondra stared at me as though she was trying to decide if I was insane. "How do you keep from taking a breath by accident?" She didn't wait for me to answer— she just put the null over her nose and mouth with the strings going around the back of her head. She tightened the strings, lifted the bowl part off her mouth long enough to take a deep breath, then picked up the board and leapt off the edge of the cliff, lying down on the board.

The top of the Bomb's Breath must've been almost even with the height of the cliff, because she sailed straight out, as if it caught her instantly. She pulled the right handle toward her and pushed the left handle away. The flaps on the side of the board moved—the right one bent down and the left one bent up—and the entire board turned until Alondra's head was toward us instead of her feet. As she got closer, she pushed the right handle and pulled the left, and turned away from us again, pushing off against the edge of the cliff with her foot. The force of her shove sent her sailing away.

I rushed to peek over the edge, afraid that there was nothing but empty air below her, but there was a wide cliff, probably a few feet below the bottom of the Bomb's Breath, and jutting out at least thirty feet. Stairs were even carved into the stone, leading back up.

Alondra caught my eye, then pushed both handles forward. The board she rode on nose-dived toward the cliff ledge below. She pulled up on both handles and it brought her head upright, and she slowly floated down until she dropped out of the Bomb's Breath. She yanked off the null, gasped for air, and grinned up at us. "That," she said, "is Sky Surfing."

Aaren sat on the ground and examined the second board as Alondra replaced her null and climbed up the stairs. He moved each of the handles, noticing how much they moved the flaps on the sides. He flipped it over to see how the mechanism that connected the handles to the flaps worked. Brock crouched down next to him, and for a while, the two of them discussed things like how the flaps affect the air and how the handles affect the flaps. I couldn't believe they could simply talk about all those technical things when they'd just seen what Alondra was able to do with one of them.

Aaren held up the null. "Do you ever let visitors who are coming to trade use these?"

Alondra shook her head. "I'm not supposed to show them to outsiders." She looked guilty for a moment. "But I'm pretty sure my dad meant I wasn't supposed to show them to adults."

Aaren looked up at me, and his smile grew bigger. "You're dying to try this right now, aren't you?"

I shrugged it off, pretending it didn't matter at all to me.

He held the board and null up. "You should test it out." He paused a moment. "For the sake of science."

I knew he added the science part just to make me feel less bad about doing something fun when we should be . . . waiting, I guessed. In truth, curiosity and excitement had grabbed me so fully, I wasn't sure I could drag myself away from this spot without Sky Surfing if I wanted to.

I pulled on the null, took a running leap off the cliff, and landed stomach-down on the board. I hung there in the air, feeling as if I wasn't even drifting downward at all. I pushed one handle forward and pulled on the other, like Alondra did, but the board tipped so suddenly, I tumbled off it, flipping from stomach to back to stomach a few times before I came to rest in the middle of the Bomb's Breath on my back.

I closed my eyes and floated, enjoying the weightlessness, even if I wasn't on the board. Then I kicked and squirmed until I was feet-down, and I drifted out of the Bomb's Breath. I landed on the cliff, pulled the null down to my neck, and let out a laugh that bounced off the cliff face. Even a total failure on the Sky Surfboard was fun. I grabbed the board when it drifted down to me, and raced up the stairs.

I handed my board and null to Brock. "You have to try this!"

Within moments, he tipped his board and fell off.

Alondra laughed and called out, "I think you tumbled even more quickly than Hope did!"

"Overachiever!" I yelled.

He gave me two thumbs up as he glided down through the Bomb's Breath.

When Brock landed on the ledge, Aaren pulled on the null and took a running leap into the air. He moved the handles a little, turning slightly toward the right. He straightened them out, then turned slightly to the left. It wasn't much, but he managed to stay on a lot longer than Brock and I did. He even figured out how to pull up on both handles and stay hanging on as he drifted to the bottom of the dense air, feetfirst.

We cheered for him the entire time. Alondra handed her board to Brock. "Here. You two go together."

I bit my lip, and looked out over the cliff's edge. After just a moment, I could see Luke's horse down below! He looked about the size of an ant, with a little tiny dust cloud rising out behind him. He was almost halfway to Downwind. We had time and nothing else to do. I looked at Brock.

He raised an eyebrow. "See who can stay on the board the longest?"

Given how quickly we'd each stayed on the board last time, it was probably the only contest we could've had. We almost crashed once by accident, then once on purpose. When I tried to shove away from the wall, I reached too far, and I flipped my board upside down. I was having so much fun, I didn't even care that I lost.

"How old do you have to be in White Rock to sky jump?" Alondra asked once I got to the top of the stairs.

I snorted, thinking about how anxious everyone in White Rock was just knowing we had sky jumped before. "Nobody but us goes into the Bomb's Breath."

"Really?" She stared at us. "Why?"

"You do realize it's deadly, right?" Brock said.

She laughed. "Yes. I realize. That's why we use the nulls, and we have to wait until our ninth birthday before we go into it. We have to be twelve before we jump without a parent, and we can never jump alone."

"I can't believe they let you at all," Aaren said.

"My dad said that when you live above the Bomb's Breath, you can either use it as a strength or accept it as a weakness. It's only a strength if you're not afraid of it." The wind blew Alondra's hair back as she grasped one of the long wooden bundles. She fitted one end into the hole at the bottom of the sky board, then bent the bundle of fabric and sticks over at a hinge close to the base. Now it looked as though the board had a six-foot-long tail. None of us even asked what it was. We just watched her work.

When she was finished, she picked up the board and

held it at her side with its tail trailing behind her. "Watch. Sky Surfing is even better with this." She placed the null over her nose and mouth, then took a running leap off the cliff, landing on her knees on the sky board, the force of her run shooting her and the board across the top of the Bomb's Breath.

When she got out far enough, she spun her board so she was facing us, then bent the hinge on the tail again, so it was sticking up like it was when she first put it in the base. She got to her feet and removed something that held the three sticks together at the top. One of the sticks stayed straight up, one fell to the right, and the other fell to the left, the cloth that was apparently attached to them spreading out tight, making a wall of fabric.

"It's a sail!" Brock yelled.

The wind caught the sail, billowing it out behind Alondra. She flew across the thirty feet of nothing but air separating her from us, and skidded to a stop on the grassy weeds right in front of me.

"See?" she said. "It's the best!"

I could hardly wait until Alondra and I finished attaching the sail to the second sky board. As soon as it was ready, I adjusted the null and took off running.

I leapt off the cliff and landed with my knees on the board. The wind rushed past my face, blowing my hair behind me as I sailed forward. None of the mountain was visible from where I knelt—I just saw miles and miles of sky all around me, with the ground far below.

When I began to slow, I tried to turn my board the same way Alondra did, but it didn't work. I panicked, my hands sweaty where I gripped the edge of the board. What if I was out farther than the edge of the lower cliff? If I drifted down through the Bomb's Breath, I'd drop out of it and fall all the way to the base of the mountain, eighty feet below.

I looked around me. This was the Bomb's Breath. My favorite place, no matter where in the world it was. My panic left, replaced with the calm that being in the Bomb's Breath always brought. Instead of turning the board around, I turned myself around so I was facing the others on the cliff. They jumped up and down and either screamed or cheered—it was hard to tell, I was so focused on my own little world.

I leaned forward and pulled up on the bundle of sticks so they were standing straight up, then got to my feet, carefully, with the sail in front of me instead of behind me like Alondra showed us. When I removed the band, the sticks fell to the sides, making the sail.

I held on tight as it propelled me toward the others. Since it had taken me longer than it had taken Alondra,

I had been drifting downward, and my board hit into the side of the cliff about a foot down from the top edge. I descended slowly, one hand on the sail. I was the captain of this ship, and I was going down with it.

While I drifted closer to the ledge below, I looked out across the Bomb's Breath. It was kind of cool to think that it went everywhere. It was the one thing that united the entire planet.

When I neared the bottom, I leapt off the board and fell feetfirst, in slow motion, until I dropped fully out of the Bomb's Breath and landed with a thump on the lower cliff. I pulled off my null, gasped for air, and screamed "Yes!" It left me feeling as though I could do anything. Maybe I could.

We each took turns after that, with Alondra teaching us new things, and us trying crazy things that even surprised her. As the afternoon sun fell lower and lower in the sky, Alondra soared up and down and around in circles, then let go of her board and did a front flip *in the Bomb's Breath* before landing on the cliff and catching her board. She had obviously spent a lot of her life practicing here. How long would it take to get that good at Sky Surfing? I would practice night and day if I lived here.

Aaren and Brock had been clapping and shouting in excitement, but I didn't realize until she landed that I hadn't said a word. I had just been sitting on the edge of the cliff, watching. Dreaming. Thinking of how it would be to live so close to a place where I could jump like this.

It also made me think about how we were enjoying the Bomb's Breath being so close, when everyone back home was probably near hysteria with worry because it was getting *too* close.

Alondra sat down next to me at the edge of the cliff, her feet dangling into the Bomb's Breath right along with mine, and we watched Brock and Aaren surf and land on the ledge. The forest spread out below us, and the stream from the waterfall meandered off to my right for miles before it wound out of view shortly after it passed Downwind. I suddenly realized that I had been having so much fun that I hadn't been watching the trail, and had no idea if I had missed them coming back.

At the sound of the gong, Alondra jumped up. "That's the dinner alert. I didn't realize we were gone so long!" We all grabbed the boards, sails, and nulls, and Alondra shoved them back into the chest. "Luke and my dad should be there. Hurry!"

# The Mines

Were we really Sky Surfing for that long? Once Alondra raced out of the woods, us trying to keep pace behind her, she slowed and walked with a straight back to the main grassy area. Everyone else in town filed in at about the same time, chatting with one another. The people in charge of food were placing platters on the tables in the front.

I couldn't believe how fully it had taken my mind off everything else. Now the two bags that I carried over my shoulder—the one with my birth mom's books and the one with the Ameiphus that I needed to trade—felt extra heavy. Probably because I hadn't been doing anything to solve either problem all afternoon.

Luke was nowhere in sight. I stood on my tippy-toes to see if he was in the crowd, but I couldn't spot his head of dark, thick hair.

"My dad isn't here, either," Alondra said, "which means he's probably in the middle of negotiations. I'm sure they'll be back soon. Let's get in line."

My shoulders slumped. Everything was taking so long!

When we all had our plates, Alondra directed us up to the table at the top center of the grassy hill. "Should we be here?" I asked. It felt as if it was reserved for her dad.

"At lunch, we eat with friends. For dinner, we eat as families." I noticed for the first time that it did look different from lunchtime. Everyone sat chatting and eating together in families, mostly at the tables instead of sprawled on the grass. "This is where we sit—well, me and my dad, since that's all who's in our family. But since you're our guests, this is your table today, too."

We all scooted in on the benches and set our plates down. I stuck my fork in the meat. I was trying to figure out what it might be, when I noticed Alondra staring at me.

"Haven't you had pork before?"

"Pork?" I asked. "What kind of an animal is a pork?"

She laughed. "It's not a 'pork,' silly. It comes from a pig."

I'd seen a picture of a pig, but I had thought that they were extinct since the bombs.

"You have pigs?" Aaren burst out. "Really?"

Alondra laughed again. "You're all so funny. They're in the livestock farms."

We ate in silence for a few minutes. I was trying not to let my anxiety show, but I could feel Alondra's eyes on me. Eventually, she said, "I'm sure they'll be back soon." She looked at me, and I glanced over at her. "Worrying won't change when they get here."

I shook out my hands. Maybe it wouldn't change anything, but that didn't stop me from worrying. Or being antsy.

"I can tell that mining is important in your town," Aaren said, clearly changing the subject to take my mind off my worries. "Does your dad work in the mines, too?"

Maybe it was the mayor's split job, the way my dad also supervised the mill back home.

"He's been the mayor for my whole life," Alondra said, "but the mines are kind of his baby." She motioned to all the people in town, seated around us. "They're everyone's baby, really. All the things that come from inside these mountains look like dusty, worthless rocks, but they're not. They're filled with treasure. Minerals and ores aren't something that you can make and they're not something you can grow. They only change as the Earth changes. The stuff in there has been there for millions of years—you just have to do the work to find it, and then it can be used for so many different things."

Hearing Alondra talk about mining made me think of rocks very differently. "Do you know much about the things you mine here?"

She looked at me as if she was offended. "I *do* pay attention in mineral studies, of course."

"Mineral studies? You have an entire class on rocks?" Aaren glanced at us, then back to Alondra. "Well, if that's the most important thing in your town, I guess that makes sense. We have a whole class on inventions."

I gasped. Alondra might know something that could help us solve the mystery my birth mom had been trying to figure out! "Do you know if any of the iron here is magnetic?"

"Nothing is magnetic anymore. The bombs didn't only affect iron—they affected all metals in that family." Alondra pointed to the statue in the clearing. "We mixed every combination of metals that came from this mountain when we made that. None of them can hold a permanent magnetic charge."

My birth mom was right! I wasn't sure how I felt about that. I was thrilled for her that her theory was correct, but at the same time, I was sad for Luke that he had been searching so long for something that didn't exist.

But like he said, there *had* to be a metal somewhere that could hold a magnetic charge. My birth mom had told Luke that she thought she could find their lost city of metal after she told him that no iron anywhere could hold a charge, so she had to believe there was another possibility. And if she was right about iron, then maybe she was right about that, too.

"Come with me," Alondra said. "I want to show you something."

I was more than happy to go with her—sitting and waiting really just meant sitting and worrying, and I didn't want to do that. We took our plates to the front table, then walked alongside Alondra up the road on the right-hand side of their pie-shaped town. Posts lined the street, and each one of them held a glass canister filled with an orange powder.

Brock walked up to one of them and squinted at it. "What are these?"

"Lights," Alondra said. "That's what we use seforium for. You need it for your Bomb's Breath?"

I told her about the earthquakes, the chemical reaction that was making the Bomb's Breath lower, and that seforium would keep it from coming down to where our houses were, making us have to leave White Rock.

"How scary!" Alondra blurted. "Is everyone going crazy? I think I'd go crazy!"

Her response made me laugh. She spoke so differently when she was around only us. "You always seem so proper when you're around other people. Are you supposed to act like that all the time?" I hoped she didn't think my question was rude.

"My dad would appreciate it if I did," Alondra said. "But no. My dad thinks a proper appearance shows that we are strong without having to trade, so that people won't manipulate us. He thinks it's important to have the upper hand. It helps that we don't need much." She gestured to everything from the homes to the mountains to the fields, the livestock farms, and the waterfall. "We'd be fine without trading. What did you bring? Food? Supplies? Relics from before the bombs?"

"Ameiphus," Aaren said. Alondra gave him a quizzical look, so he continued. "It cures Shadel's Sickness."

Alondra's eyes grew big. "We don't have that kind of medicine." She walked in silence for a long time. Eventually, she said, "My mom died from Shadel's."

"All my grandparents died from it, too," I said, "before Aaren's mom discovered the medicine."

"So people in White Rock don't die from it anymore?"

"No," I said. "They don't die from other infections, either."

Alondra walked in silence for a dozen paces, then shook her head, as though she was trying to shake off memories of her mom's death. "You seemed interested in minerals and ores, so I thought I'd show you some of the mines."

Alondra walked us past the town's three rows of homes, every single one of them made out of stone. About three-fourths of the way up the road, we started seeing holes in the cliff face, of all different sizes, that were openings to mines for various minerals and metals. She stopped outside the fourth mine, picked up a hanging lantern filled with the same orange powder as the ball in the statue and the lanterns lining the streets, and shook it. The powder began to glow a brilliant orange.

"The seforium really does that?" I asked.

"It only glows when you mix it with another mineral," Alondra said as she showed us inside the mine. "They separate over time, though, so every few hours you have to give it a shake. What do you use for light if you don't have seforium?"

"White phosphorus in clear jars, powered by electrolyte batteries," Aaren said. "Or sometimes regular lanterns with fuel and a wick that you light. But these are so much brighter."

When our eyes adjusted to the orange light, Alondra said, "This is the gypsum mine."

We stood in a cavern with walls of gray stone. Alondra walked near the end of the mine, held up the lantern, and scraped a rock with her fingernail. It came off easily.

"It looks like sugar that got moisture in the container and clumped together," I said.

Alondra smiled. "It dissolves in water, too. We put some in the soil in our cornfields, we use it to make the walls inside our houses, and we make toothpaste out of it."

"Really?" Aaren said. "You brush your teeth with rocks?"

Alondra laughed and put her hand on Aaren's shoulder. "You're so funny."

"Was this always gypsum?" I asked. "Or was it something different before the bombs?"

"Always gypsum." Her eyes sparkled in the light of the lantern. "But the seforium's new since the bombs. Do you want to see that mine?" She led us out of the gypsum mine and over some rocky, uneven ground littered with boulders as we rounded the rise of mountain at our right.

She stepped into a cave whose opening wasn't much

taller than me. "The seam isn't very wide, so this cave is a lot smaller than some of the others."

The cave was short enough that I could touch the top of it if I stood on my tiptoes. Alondra held the lantern as high as she could, and I reached out and ran my fingers over the orange stone at the back. It was jagged here, but smooth in a few places. My fingers got an orange powder on them from rubbing it.

"This is what'll save us," I breathed out, my voice barely a whisper.

# Missing Pieces

I stared at the orange rock, nestled among other rocks, showing through in some places and mostly hidden in others. "My birth mom was trying to figure out what was the same between minerals and ores that were transformed by the bombs. She kept a book." I pulled Anna's notebook from my bag and showed Alondra one of the pages. "Every time she found a rock that had been changed, she recorded it in here. But she didn't have seforium listed. Can you help us figure out what she would've written about it?"

Alondra held the light closer and squinted at the page. "Yeah. I learned this in mineral studies two years ago."

We walked outside the cave and sat in a circle in the middle of the rocks and dirt. After finding my pencil in the bottom of my bag, I handed it and the notebook to Alondra. She opened to the first blank page; then, flipping between the blank page and the one before it, Alondra filled out the information in the same way for seforium.

When she finished, she placed the notebook in the center of our little circle, and we all stared at it.

"Nothing." Aaren stood up and walked a few steps away. "That didn't give us any new clues at all."

I rested my elbows on my knees and pushed my hands through my hair. There had to be something. Something we were missing.

"Maybe it doesn't matter what type of rock it is," Brock said. "Or what kinds of crystals form while it's being made. Or how fast the new mineral was created. Maybe none of the facts in the books even matter."

Alondra stood up. "But those kinds of things *do* matter! They're what make a mineral or ore have the properties it has. Like on the periodic table of elements—"

Alondra stopped talking when Aaren snatched the notebook from my hands. "The periodic chart! Do you remember how Mr. Hudson wrote in all the minerals and ores that were new since the bombs?"

"He didn't write them all on one side," Brock said. "They were in random spots around the page."

I nodded and opened the textbook to the charts in the back, stopping at the periodic table of elements. It was a colorful chart that showed every element that existed before the bombs, each in its own box.

"Maybe it wasn't random." Aaren paged through Anna's notebook and stopped on a page with an odd-shaped rock that looked somewhat crystal-like. "I remember seeing the name of this one listed on Mr. Hudson's periodic table right here." He pointed to an empty spot, then scanned through the properties of the rock that Anna had written in. "Yes! It shares some of the same properties as the others in that column! Maybe Mr. Hudson put them in specific places on the chart because that's where they're supposed to go. That's what the periodic chart does—it puts ones that are similar in the same row or column. See? All of the metals that can hold a magnetic charge are on the same row. Do you remember where seforium was on the chart?"

I squeezed my eyes shut, and thought back to that night when Mr. Hudson showed us what was happening to the Bomb's Breath. He had pointed right at seforium on the chart. "In the blank row between the top chunk and the bottom chunk," I said. "In the middle? Maybe?"

"I think so," Aaren said.

All my birth mom's notes started clicking into place in my mind. "Alondra, seforium was something before the bombs, right? Do you know what it used to be?"

"Yes. We talked about it for a whole class period once. It was hassium." She leaned over and pointed at it on the chart. "But hassium didn't actually exist before the bombs, either. It was more . . ." Alondra shrugged. "A concept. Something they could only make in a lab, but it wasn't very stable. The bombs made the hassium; then the side effects of the bombs changed it almost instantly into the seforium, which *is* stable."

Hassium was on the chart right above where Mr. Hudson had written in seforium. "But what does it mean that they're by each other?"

Aaren stood up and started pacing. "If seforium is right below hassium, then it's because when hassium changed, it gave some of its properties to seforium."

Alondra stood up, too, biting her lip.

Brock and I just looked at each other. I felt as if we were on the very edge of figuring things out, but couldn't quite get there. My mind was running through everything I'd read, but as soon as I'd almost think of something, a giant stone wall went up in my mind that I couldn't get around. I left the book sitting on my lap and leaned back on my hands, staring up at the darkening sky.

This was useless. Even with Alondra's help, we didn't know enough about rocks to figure this out. I dropped my head back and closed my eyes.

Then I jerked upright. "Which properties did hassium give it?"

Aaren froze for a moment, then opened the notebook and compared it to the textbook on my lap. "A similar electron grouping."

If hassium gave some of its properties to the element right below it . . . I moved my finger to the top of that very same column. Then maybe iron transferred some of its properties to the element right below it, too. I moved my finger from the box that read "Iron," sliding it down one. "When metals change, they move in the same direction," I mumbled, repeating my birth mom's theory.

"Yes!" Aaren shouted. "That's it!"

I looked up at him. "Anna was talking about moving in the same direction on the periodic chart!"

The four of us crowded around the book while Aaren flipped to the page about iron. He jabbed his finger at the same list of properties. "Iron had a unique electron arrangement that made it magnetic. The one below it, ruthenium, had a slightly different arrangement, which is why it *wasn't* magnetic."

"They're in the same column," Brock said. "So if

hassium gave some of its properties to the element below it, then iron would've given some of its properties to the one below it as well."

I turned back to the periodic table of elements.

"So if we wanted a metal with iron's magnetic properties . . . ," Brock said.

Alondra put her finger on the square with iron, then slid it down one. "Then you need to move down one to ruthenium."

Aaren grinned. "And if someone can find ruthenium—"

"Then," I said, "they'll have found a metal that can hold a permanent magnetic charge!"

# 28 Lost

"So where do we find ruthenium?" I asked Alondra.

She shrugged. "I've seen it on the periodic chart, but we never talk about it in class. We only talk about the ones we have around here."

Aaren flipped to ruthenium in the book. "It looks like it hasn't been found anywhere in the United States."

I dropped my head. I had been so excited to tell Luke what we'd figured out. Apparently, it was just another dead end that made us *think* we'd solved something but really wasn't helpful at all. "It doesn't matter. That's not what we are here for." As soon as I said it, all the anxiety that had gone away while we'd been working on finding a solution returned in full force.

Brock squinted at the sun as the last bit of it dipped behind the mountain. "We'd better head back."

I pushed the textbook and notebook into my bag.

It was getting more difficult to see in the darkness. As we hurried toward the grassy hill, a few people walked up the road, stopping at each seforium light. They'd pull a lever that tipped the cylinder up and down, and then the orange powder started glowing. Someone walked up to the sculpture in the clearing and gave the glass ball a spin, and it suddenly blazed the same orange hue, almost as it had during the day when the sun shone on it. The entire town glowed like sunset, making it feel warm. Like it was lit by firelight.

There was no sign of Luke or the mayor, which made me even more antsy, and made me realize that we'd spent *hours* here. Hours during daylight, when we weren't on the road, trying to get back in time. Brock plopped down on one of the benches attached to the tables, and the rest of us joined him. Judging by everyone's faces, the excitement at figuring out Anna's theories had worn off. We were all thinking about the dangers back home.

I hoped that Luke had gotten a lot of opportunities to talk with the mayor on their trip back to Heaven's Reach, and that he had already talked him into trading us the seforium. They'd been gone a long time—maybe

I wouldn't end up having to negotiate at all. Maybe they'd have it all worked out, and we'd be ready to leave as soon as they got here.

I stood up when I saw movement by the clearing out of the corner of my eye. It was Luke and another man. Based on the man's coppery-colored hair and the way he walked tall with his shoulders back and his hands clasped behind him, I knew he must be the mayor. But Luke stopped just at the edge of the woods. The mayor kept walking through the clearing, glanced up at us, then turned and went into the main building.

My stomach dropped. Something was wrong.

I ran down the hill and through the clearing. "Luke," I called out.

His shoulders were stiff, his hands were clenched into fists at his sides, and he glared toward the weeds at his feet. I stepped right in front of him. He finally looked up.

"The mayor is furious. He asked me to leave."

I stared at him in shock. "What? Why? What happened?"

"During the entire trip back," Luke said, "I talked to him about trading the Ameiphus for seforium and iron. And he's such a stubborn—" He ground his teeth. "He wouldn't say yes. He just kept going on about the iron being dangerous and difficult to mine. I tried everything. When nothing else worked, I pointed out that he could've saved his wife from dying of Shadel's Sickness if he'd had Ameiphus, and was he really not going to save the rest of his town from that same fate? Somehow, he took that as an attack on his character, and told me he doesn't want me in his town."

*"And iron?"* Everything started to spin and I couldn't get enough air. My brain wouldn't connect any thoughts together, except the only words I managed to hear him say. "You asked the mayor to trade the Ameiphus for seforium *and* iron?"

The anger left his face, and his eyes changed to pleading. "The iron he has is really important. This whole town is one of the farthest places from where any green bombs hit, so it may be unaffected by the bombs. But not only that, this iron was *inside a mountain*. You can't get more protected than that. This could be our lost city of metal."

"It's *not* the lost city of metal. Anna was right—there's no iron anywhere that'll work."

Luke's eyes flashed to mine. I saw the pain on his face. But I was so angry that he had cared about iron more than he cared about saving my town, and so afraid that we might not get seforium without his help, I didn't care. "We're here because the Bomb's Breath is coming down

214

in White Rock, and we need to stop it. Now we might not be able to at all." My voice came out fierce and trembling.

"Hope, it's not possible to stop it. We left White Rock thirteen days ago. Even if we hadn't run into a storm and no one got injured, there would be no way to make it back in eight days. The Bomb's Breath will lower to the height where the earth is cracked, and it will stay there. Your town will have to leave White Rock and live somewhere else. Nothing we do here will change that. Not even if you did get the mayor to give you the seforium and a trailer to haul it home in. I'm sorry. But with the iron, we could've changed the world."

I couldn't hear this. Sadness and fear and hopelessness and anger filled me so full I thought I might burst. This couldn't be the end. We couldn't have failed.

He gazed into the woods for several long moments, then looked back at me. "Maybe we should've turned around long ago. Especially since I knew I'd let you down in the end." He put his hand on my shoulder. "I'm going to miss you."

His focus shifted away to Brock, Aaren, and Alondra, then to me again. "People from your town will come for you. The mayor's a piece of work, but he'll let you stay here and look out for you until they arrive."

Then he turned and walked away.

My feet were frozen to the ground. I couldn't even make them move to run after him. He just disappeared through the trees.

Brock, Aaren, and Alondra came up behind me, but I still had my eyes on the woods.

"Are you okay?" Aaren asked.

Soon, the Bomb's Breath would be low enough to touch my house. We were five hundred miles away, missing almost all of the people we came with, including the person who was probably my only blood relative on Earth, we had no trailer, not even the smallest pebble of seforium, and the only one who could give it to us was furious. I was very much not okay.

I wondered at what point my dad would realize that we'd failed, and that we weren't going to make it back in time. Would my parents keep watching for us every day? Would they worry that something happened and I wouldn't make it back at all? I could feel the ticking down of time like a heartbeat.

I wished there was some way to talk to them. I clutched my necklace in my fist. Suddenly, I missed them so much my gut hurt.

And strangely, I wished I could talk to Luke. I wanted to ask why. I wanted to ask how he could leave me when we barely found each other.

He told me that I was persistent. That I didn't give up when everyone else would have, and that even if I didn't have the tools I needed, I had something in me that'd work anyway. But how did all that matter when what I needed to do wasn't even possible?

So many thoughts spun circles in my mind, I couldn't focus. As if I reached out and picked one of them at random, I blurted, "It's too late."

Brock and Aaren looked at each other, like maybe I was broken.

"Luke says it's impossible to make it back in time," I said. "We can't save White Rock."

"So it's over?" Aaren asked. "We lost?"

"Yeah," I said. "I guess we did."

# A Different Tool

We lost. The four of us stared at the ground for a long time, not saying a word. At first, I accepted that we lost. Then, after a while, I didn't anymore. We *couldn't* have lost. Not after all we had gone through.

Luke had said that there was nothing we could do to change things. But as a town, we had changed what happened next in our history when the bandits invaded. That had seemed impossible at the time, but it wasn't. This couldn't be impossible now.

We needed to change things. To find a way that wasn't impossible.

I took a deep breath. "We need a way to get home with the seforium, and we need to do it in eight days or less."

"But how?" Aaren asked. "It took us thirteen days to get here *without* the seforium. With it, a trailer will be heavy. We can't make the horses go faster."

"Can we get home without the horses?" I asked.

"Yeah. By magic," Brock said. "Or maybe Alondra has an airplane from before the bombs whose metal didn't collapse in on itself, and we can fly home."

"That's not helping," I said.

"You're serious?" Brock asked. "How are we supposed to come up with a way to get home more quickly?"

"You two are the inventors," I said. "*Invent* a way." I sighed. "I guess I'm the negotiator. I'll be off negotiating."

They both gave me looks of pity. "Don't," I said. Then Alondra and I trudged back toward the mayor's office, Brock and Aaren not far behind us, and I told her what had happened with her dad and Luke. There was a dark heaviness in my gut that had gotten worse every time I thought of this moment since we left the ruins. But all along I hadn't imagined the circumstances would be this bad. I couldn't afford to feel sorry for myself or to panic now. There wasn't anyone else to take my spot, and now that Luke was gone, there wasn't anyone to help me.

"Hope," Aaren said, "you're not by yourself," like I said to him before he performed his first solo surgery on Cass. "You've got us."

I swallowed hard. "Thanks."

We left Aaren and Brock at the grass, and Alondra walked beside me to the door in the main building that her dad had gone into. "Do you think Luke will be coming back?" she asked.

I thought about how final his goodbye felt, and shook my head. "He's gone."

When I stopped in front of the mayor's closed door, Alondra put a hand on my arm. "I know my dad, Hope. He prides himself on making good decisions for this town, and Luke challenged that. Luke was also dishonest about what your town needed, and my dad values honesty more than anything else. Just . . . keep that in mind."

I took a deep breath, trying to remember all the things that everyone suggested, but half of it jumbled in my brain and the other half didn't seem to be there at all. I squared my shoulders and knocked. Then I wiped my sweaty hands on my pants a few times while I waited for the mayor.

When he opened the door, Alondra said, "Dad, this is my friend Hope. Her dad is the council head of White Rock."

"Hello, Hope," Mayor Alvey said. "Come in." His mouth was tight, and his arms were crossed. He walked over to his desk, leaned against it, and motioned for me to sit down, so I did. Alondra left, shutting the door behind her, and we were alone.

My mind went back to every time I'd been in this situation—every time I tried to talk myself out of detention. The time I wanted to talk my teacher into letting me put my broken invention in the Harvest Festival and couldn't even open my mouth. The time I tried to talk the council into letting us search for Ameiphus outside the crater. I could think of what to say in my head, but the words always got away before they reached my mouth. Maybe I needed to plow ahead faster, before the words could escape.

"Luke's gone," I said, "but we still need the seforium, and we still have the Ameiphus to trade—Luke told you all about it, right? And we don't need the iron. Actually, we never needed that, and he didn't tell me that he was trying to get you to give it to him. All we need is the seforium. Enough of it to save my town, which is a lot, I know."

"You're nervous," Mayor Alvey said.

I nodded, and reminded myself that I wasn't alone. Aaren, Brock, and Alondra weren't far away, and they were rooting for me. But even though I wasn't alone, it didn't mean I knew what to say to try to talk him into trading with us.

Suddenly, my mind was back at the river, with Luke

telling me about my birth grandpa, and how he always said, *If you don't have a wrench, use needle-nose pliers.* Is this what he meant? I didn't have negotiating skills, so I needed to use a skill I did have instead. What skill could I use? None of mine worked for this.

"Luke was dishonest and manipulative," the mayor said in a voice made of stone. "So how am I supposed to think you'll be any more truthful than he was? How should I believe anything you say? How do I know that the medicine is even real?"

I ducked under the strap of the bag that Mr. Williams had given me and held it out to the mayor. "No, it's real! See?" I unfastened the flap and opened the bag to show him the blue medicine inside.

He didn't even look in the bag—he just kept his eyes on me, his forehead scrunched. "How do I trust that it's not fake and doesn't really do anything? And the Bomb's Breath isn't lowering here—why should I believe that it's lowering inside White Rock? Or that you're even from White Rock? Luke certainly isn't. For all I know, you three are orphans he found on the Forbidden Flats, and you all concocted this story to get me to hand over one of our most precious resources—our ability to make light."

I was speechless. It never even occurred to me that the mayor might think we were making it up. Did I have any proof? We had almost nothing with us! Nothing that would prove that the medicine was real or that I was from White Rock. In fact, with as little as we had, the mayor's orphan story was sounding more and more realistic than the truth.

I couldn't think of any way to get him to believe a thing I said.

An idea suddenly popped into my head. "Come with me," I said. "I can prove I'm from White Rock."

We walked out of his office, and I didn't see Brock, Aaren, or Alondra. I didn't let myself even wonder if that was a good thing or a bad thing; I just headed straight for the woods. As we walked, I told him everything I could think of about Aaren's mom discovering Ameiphus, and what kinds of illnesses it cured. About how we used to only search for it in the woods inside White Rock, but that after the bandits attacked during the winter, we decided to hunt for it outside our crater. I told him about the earthquake while I was in the tree, and Mr. Hudson's calculation about the Bomb's Breath coming down, how much my town was freaking out, how hard it was for my dad to let me leave to come here, and about our trip and the storm and the rest of my group. I knew I was rambling, but people only rambled when they were telling the truth, right?

The mayor listened the entire time. He didn't ask questions, but he also didn't look as though he believed me.

When we reached the clearing where Alondra had taken us Sky Surfing, I took both of my bags off my shoulders, laid them on the ground, and said, "Watch." Then I moved back from the edge quite a bit, and took off running toward it.

As soon as I did, the mayor yelled, panicked, "You're not wearing a null!"

That was kind of the point.

I sprinted right to the cliff, took a big gulp of air, leapt off the edge, and did a front flip. Since the edge of the cliff wasn't any higher than the Bomb's Breath, I only completed half of the flip before I hit the compressed air, lying flat on my back. For a moment, I ignored the mayor and every problem that we had and just floated, my arms and legs stretched out, looking up at the moonlit sky with the clouds that were floating the same as me.

There wasn't anyone to tell me when I was nearing the bottom of the Bomb's Breath and I didn't want to take any chances that I'd fall onto the ledge flat on my back, so I pulled my arms and legs into a ball, then pushed my feet out toward the ground. When I landed, I caught my breath and looked up at the mayor, who was staring over the edge in shock and disbelief. I smiled, jogged to the stairs, felt for the air, took a deep breath, then climbed back up to him.

"There is nowhere on the Forbidden Flats between White Rock and here high enough to reach the Bomb's Breath. The only way I would've learned to do that was if I lived in White Rock."

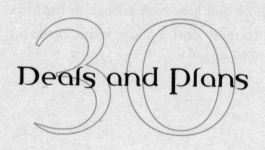

# Deals and Plans

Mayor Alvey didn't say anything, so I kept talking. "I'm sorry that Luke said those things, and that he lied to you about what we needed. I didn't know he was going to. And the medicine really does work. It saved a lot of people in my town who would've died from Shadel's. And last winter when bandits invaded my town and shot my dad, it saved him, too." My voice cracked at the end, remembering how pale my dad's face had looked and how hot his skin was while he was lying in the clinic in White Rock before he had gotten the medicine.

The mayor stared out across the Forbidden Flats for a moment. Finally, he said, "I believe you."

I grinned all the way to my ears. "So does that mean you'll trade?"

"Metals and minerals aren't like plants. If you use them up, you can't just grow more. There's a finite amount."

I held my breath.

"And because of that," he said, "it's our responsibility to share. We'll make the trade, and get you a cart so your horses can pull it home."

"Really?" I jumped up and yelled "Yes!" so loud that Aaren, Brock, and Alondra probably heard it wherever they were. "Thank you!"

I couldn't believe I did it! Not the way Luke would've done it and not the way my dad would've. I did it my own way. I used pliers instead of a wrench, like my birth grandpa used to say.

The mayor and I walked back through the woods, the moon lighting our way, and this time he did all the talking. He mostly spoke about finding the beauty that's in the Earth itself, when it looks so rough at first, and respecting the mountains that provided it all.

"I think my birth mom felt that way, too," I said.

The mayor looked at me differently, as if he was meeting me for the first time.

"I've been studying her notes about minerals and ores

that were changed by the bombs," I said. "We've been trying to come up with some theories, but it didn't work out so well."

"Sometimes it doesn't," the mayor said, holding a skinny tree branch up high enough for me to walk under.

I ducked under the branch right as it occurred to me that Anna believed they—her dad, Luke, and her—could find the lost city of metal. Not that it existed somewhere in the world, but that it existed someplace where they could find it.

"Mayor Alvey," I said, "if a book says that a mineral has only been found in another country, does that mean that is the only place it is?"

"Not at all. It means it hasn't been found here *yet*. There are plenty of minerals that were thought to be in only one location until people searched for them and found them. What are you looking for?"

"Ruthenium."

"Ahh." The mayor looked thoughtful for a few moments, then said, "It would be found in rock formed by pressure and heat—metamorphic rock—which is buried far beneath the surface. It wouldn't be easy to find."

"But there's a chance?"

He shrugged. "Possibly."

There was a chance. Somehow, that was enough, if

for no other reason than it meant that my birth mom had been right. "Thank you," I said.

"I wish you much success in all your future research on mineral theories."

When we neared the orange glow from the seforium lamps in the clearing, I saw Alondra drop an armful of rope and Aaren and Brock set down a bunch of long sticks. The three of them looked at us with expectant faces.

I took the bag of Ameiphus off my shoulders and handed it to the mayor. "Thank you for saying yes."

He nodded once and shook my hand. "And thank you for the medicine."

I turned to Aaren, Brock, and Alondra. "Did you come up with a plan?"

They all beamed, which felt like flying all over again. I knew they'd invent something.

"Well," Brock said, "first we thought about making some kind of carrier with wings. Or using the river. We even talked about using a hot-air balloon."

Alondra cut in, her voice as excited as Brock's. "But seforium is too heavy for flying, the river flows the wrong direction, and according to Aaren, hot-air balloons are unpredictable, don't usually move forward fast, and only work in the morning hours."

"The ruins were at the halfway point, right?" Aaren asked, and I nodded. "It took us nine days to get there, but it only took us a little less than four more days to get here. If we went home as fast as we traveled that second half of the way here, we'd make it in time."

"We made it that fast because we weren't pulling the trailer anymore," I said. "But the horses will have to pull a cart on the way back. It'll be just as slow."

"Unless," Alondra said, "you don't have to use horses to pull the cart. Then they can go just as fast as they did that last part of your trip."

"It was the sails on the Sky Surfboards that gave us the idea," Brock said. "Well, that and talking to Luke by the river that one night."

"The wind in Desolation Alley!" I yelled as my brain caught up.

Brock and Aaren grinned.

"Yep, Desolation Alley," Aaren said. "The bridge to cross over the river isn't far from here. All we need is a sail, and with the cart"—he paused and gave the mayor a thank-you nod—"the wind can push us home."

"And the sail?" I asked.

"That's what these sticks are for," Brock said. "To make the frame. We can use the blankets from our bedrolls for the fabric. We won't need the sails at night and we don't need the blankets during the day."

I guessed spending two hours a day in inventions class back home was a good thing. Even if I hated it.

The mayor walked over to the big metal gong by the tables and hit it six times—one long, two short, two long, then one short—as if he was playing a song, but then at the end, all the notes muddled together into one. I looked to Alondra and raised an eyebrow. She said, "That's the call for the people who work in the lumber mill."

Huh. "Do you have codes for every job?" I asked.

Alondra nodded. "One gong for everyone, two for only the adults, three for just the kids, and a song for each of the different places to work."

"Wow," I said. "A way to communicate. That's pretty cool."

Four people joined us on the grassy area, and the mayor turned to one of them. "We need a four-by-seven cart. They'll need a post right in the center that they can connect this frame to."

Brock jumped up. "I'll help."

The mayor nodded to Brock, and Brock dashed off with the four others to the lumber mill. Aaren and Alondra started laying out the long sticks they had cut.

The gong sounded, and Alondra looked up as her dad banged a song on it. "Mine workers. Probably to get the seforium ready." A moment later, he banged a different song. "Doctor," Alondra said before either of us asked. "She'll probably want to talk to you, Aaren, about how to use the Ameiphus."

Aaren looked at me, like he was wondering why I hadn't started helping yet, but I hadn't been able to move since I pictured everything together. The carts I'd seen here had a third axle in front. We could steer by having someone sit on the left and someone on the right, with our feet pushing on the axle, but Luke said that the wind in Desolation Alley didn't go the whole way. For the last 125 miles, we'd need two horses to pull the cart, so they'd have to come with us. Two people to drive the cart; two people to ride the horses.

It wasn't just that I wasn't ready to give up on Luke—we *needed* him for the trip back. And I had no idea where he was.

# Downwind

I tried to think where Luke might have gone. His home in Arris was too far to go without supplies. Because of what I guessed he had in his saddlebags, Glacier and even the ruins were out, also.

Then it hit me. He went to Downwind. They made trades there, so surely he could get the supplies he needed. Alondra said it was about an hour's ride away. It was risky to go searching for him there, but too much was at stake not to try.

"When do you think the sail will be finished?" I asked Aaren.

"Probably a couple of hours. We'll leave as soon as it gets light enough to see in the morning."

Then I needed to catch up to Luke right now.

I cleared my throat. "We have to have four people for this to work. We need Luke. I've got to go find him."

"What?" Aaren squeaked. "Are you crazy? It's dark and you don't know where he is!"

"I'll be careful, I promise. Keep working on the sails, and I'll be back by the time you're done."

I hurried across the clearing, descended the stairs through the Bomb's Breath, and raced down the pathway to the bottom of the mountain. When I got to the place where the horses were tied up, I saddled Arabelle. In only a few minutes, we were galloping toward Downwind.

There weren't as many trees here, so I could see Downwind, the metal of the buildings glowing silver in the moonlight, almost the entire way. The closer I got, the more remnants of homes I came across. A few even had all four walls intact. I wondered if people lived in them. Probably not—people needed towns for protection from bandits. Then I wondered if bandits lived in them, and suddenly all the deeper shadows looked spooky. I pushed Arabelle faster.

I headed for the area where a lot of buildings lay on top of each other with space in the middle—that was probably where they lived.

After nearly an hour of riding, I went around the first building in my path. It was flat on its side, like a tree that had fallen over. Except it was forty feet high lying down. I looked up in awe of how tall it was—of how wide it used to be before it fell. I zigzagged around the next few buildings.

Everywhere I looked, I saw some strange black rocks that were flat on the top. Wherever a building lay, the big black rocks were around it. Always flat. When I came upon a building where there were a ton of the rocks, some of them almost as wide as me, my curiosity got the best of me. Even though I was in a hurry, I pulled Arabelle to a stop and jumped down to get a better look. I squinted in the small amount of light. It wasn't one big flat rock. It was a bunch of pebbles, held together by blackish stuff that was similar to a rock, but softer.

I gasped when everything clicked in my mind. "This is pavement!" I said to no one.

Mr. Allen, my history teacher, had told us that the roads used to be covered with this stuff before the bombs. I wished Aaren and Brock were here to see it. I picked up a broken chunk and shoved it in my bag, so I could get a closer look when it was light. Then I took off riding again.

For a mile or so, the fallen buildings were easy to go around. Then I got to the part I'd seen from Heaven's Reach—the buildings formed a wall around where the people lived—and I couldn't find a way past it. The buildings were so big, I couldn't go over them. Because of how they had all fallen, I couldn't go under them, either. And they were touching, so I couldn't go around them. Only the moon lit my path, which didn't help matters at all.

After almost an hour of going around the perimeter, I finally saw an entrance. One building had fallen on another, and the bottom building was squished, but not all the way. It left a triangle of space underneath the top building that was about five feet at the highest point. But the building that had smashed the other was so big! I looked up at it. "What do you think, Arabelle? If we go under, is it going to fall on us?" She sidestepped a little and snorted. Was that a yes or a no? I looked farther along the perimeter, but this was the only way in that I could see.

I slid off Arabelle and patted her side. "It's going to be a tight squeeze, but don't worry. You'll make it through." I hoped. I held her reins, and went into the opening first. Arabelle had to drop her head to fit in behind me.

The building seemed even bigger once I was under it.

I tried to not look up—to only focus on the moonlight at the end of the tunnel, if you could call it a tunnel. "Fifty more feet," I told Arabelle. Then, "Twenty more feet and we're out. Keep coming. It's okay."

A wave of relief washed over me once we made it through and back under a starry sky.

And then someone grabbed me.

# Captured

"Let go of me!" I yelled. There were four of them, all dressed in brown leather and holding guns. "I'm not a bandit!"

One of the men, who looked as though he might be the boss of them, said, "Who are you here with?"

"Nobody. It's only me."

"How old are you?"

"Twelve."

"You expect me to believe that a twelve-year-old girl came here, in the dark, all by herself?"

"I'll be thirteen in a few months!" I called out, hoping it would help.

"Take her to holding. Keep a good eye out for whoever she came with."

"I'm looking for my uncle! I think he might be here. His name is Luke."

Two of them grabbed me by the arms and started pushing me down a pathway that bordered enormous gardens while the fourth guy—the boss—went over to Arabelle and grasped her reins. They steered me along a dirt road next to one of the buildings, and I tried to explain why I was there.

I stopped talking when we walked out of a grove of cherry trees. A large building came into the moonlit view that was unlike anything I had seen before. It was made of cement, but not solid cement. A row of cement lay on the ground, then a row of emptiness above that, then a cement row, then an empty row—five layers of cement high, and each of the layers was held up by cement pillars.

I said to the nicer of the two men, "What is that?"

"It's a parking garage."

I blinked at him a few times.

"People used to park their cars in there before the bombs."

"You don't worry about it falling?"

"No. It's all cement—it's as sturdy as they come, which is why most of us have built our homes in there."

The other man glared at him and pushed me toward a stone and brick building at the back corner of the square.

Four giant columns stood in front of the building, with lion heads carved into the stone at the top of each one. I could tell this wasn't just built before the bombs, it was built a very long time before them. We walked into a lobby with floors made of flat stone and mammoth pillars holding up a high ceiling. This was a fancy place. Not somewhere to take prisoners. I expected them to let me go sit on one of the benches against the back wall to wait, but the man shoved me down a hall at the left.

"I don't have much time!" I begged. "I have to find my uncle. My entire town is depending on it."

Both men ignored me, even the nicer one, and shoved me into a room. I tried to run back out before they shut the door, but they were quick, and I heard the click of the lock. I waited a moment, hoping that they had walked away, then tried the knob.

Locked.

I shook the handle and pulled and kicked at it, and even ran my shoulder into the door. I looked around. There wasn't a window to try to escape through. Not a single piece of furniture, either. Nothing! I banged against the door and yelled "Help me!" I banged and screamed until I was so exhausted I collapsed onto the floor. Then I stared up at the ceiling, wondering how I was ever going to get myself out of this mess.

I sat up straight at the sound of the door opening. Someone heard me!

It was the boss man. Then he opened the door wider and I saw Luke standing next to him. A rush of so many emotions hit me, I couldn't even tell if I was happy or mad. I got to my feet.

The boss man left and Luke gave me a half-smile. He kind of looked amused. I didn't know if he was amused that I had come—that I had known where to find him—or that I was locked in this room. But he also looked sad. Maybe he was sad that I came.

"I should've known you'd figure out where I went," Luke said. "You're a smart girl."

"I'm smart enough to know that running away isn't the answer."

Luke stood still and silent.

"You used me. And you didn't care if the consequences hurt my town."

"I cared, I just—"

"But we still need you."

He shook his head. "You're better off without me." He walked toward the door. "I'll get them to let you out of here so you can head back."

"Remember that day we talked by the river?" My voice came out quietly enough that I wondered if he heard me. But then he froze, his hand on the door.

Still facing the door, he said, "Yeah."

"Because of you, I used my needle-nose pliers."

He spun around and looked at me.

"I talked the mayor into giving us the seforium and a cart."

His eyebrows shot up. "You're going to try to make it back in time?"

"We *are* going to make it back in time, if you come with us. Aaren, Brock, and Alondra are making a sail. We have everything we need to go back home through Desolation Alley, except a fourth person."

"You can't rely on me, Hope. I've never been someone *anyone* could rely on."

"But that doesn't change the fact that we're family, and family doesn't give up on each other. Everyone makes mistakes. You didn't think of giving up on your sister when she made a mistake, so why should I give up on you?"

"You'd get in a lot less trouble without me."

I shrugged. "Probably."

He looked at me for a long while. Finally, he let out a deep breath and said, "You know how I told you that you're persistent?"

"Yeah."

"I don't like it when you use it on me."

I held my breath, trying to figure out what that meant.

"Let's get you out of here," he said. "We need to go back to White Rock."

Luke got us back to Heaven's Reach on a much faster route than the one I'd traveled.

At the top of the mountain path, in the clearing before Heaven's Reach, he reminded me that the mayor didn't want him there, and told me he was going to sleep with our horses.

When I stepped around the building and onto the grass, I saw the others working under the orange glow of the seforium lamps in the grassy area. Brock and Aaren rushed forward to meet me.

"Don't do that again," Brock said.

I crinkled my forehead. "What?"

"You left! All by yourself, and you were gone for hours! We didn't know where you went, so we didn't know where to start looking for you."

"I'm sorry," I said. "I didn't want you to be worried—"

"Not knowing was much worse, because then we had to worry about *everywhere* you could be," Aaren said.

"Hope, if something had happened to you . . ." Brock let his sentence trail off, which made me think about all the terrible things that could've happened. And if I was wrong and Luke hadn't been in Downwind, I'd still be locked up there, and they wouldn't know where to find me.

I swallowed. "It would've been bad."

"Did you find him?" Aaren asked.

"Yep. He's with the horses. He's going with us."

"That's good," Brock said, "because . . ."—he drew out the word and motioned to the sail with a flourish—"we finished!"

The sail was on the grass, all of our bedding laid out like puzzle pieces across it, with rope tied to the frame but not yet tied to the corners of each blanket.

"And . . . ," Brock said, motioning toward a cart filled to the top of its two-foot sides with the orange mineral. "Ta-da!" A wooden shaft rose from the center a few inches above the seforium, to slide the sail frame into.

"We have the seforium," I said. We all took a moment and stood around the cart, feeling light enough to fly. After the past few days—or really, the past thirteen days—I couldn't believe we actually, finally had it.

"And food, too," Brock said as he gestured to two bundles nestled among the mineral.

"We leave first thing in the morning," Aaren said.

I could hardly wait.

# Desolation Alley

The sky was barely beginning to lighten, and I was wide awake. We were heading home today!

After we ate breakfast, we tied our bedding to the straps on the sail's frame. The sun hadn't yet risen when Brock left with the cart down a small canyon near the mines that had a road wide enough for the cart to go to the base of the mountain. Aaren, Alondra, and I carried the sail down the path we always used.

By the time we made it through all the switchbacks in the path and got to the bottom, we heard a rumbling from the other direction, and turned to see Brock and a man from Heaven's Reach riding the cart down the incline. They sat on a bench the lumber workers had added to the front, and each had their feet on one side of the axle. It came to a stop not far from us.

Luke came out to meet us, holding the reins to both Ruben and Buck.

I gasped. "We can only take two horses! What are we going to do with the other two?" There had been so many problems to worry about, I hadn't even thought of this one.

"We're taking Luke's horse and Arabelle with us," Aaren said. "The people here are going to take care of Ruben and Buck."

"We'll treat them well," Alondra said.

It hit me then that I might not ever see her again. "Thank you," I said. "For everything."

She curtsied. "I think you make an excellent Sky Surfer."

I grinned. "You too."

She glanced from Luke to me. "I'm surprised your uncle came back."

I shrugged. "I think he's more loyal than he thought he was."

She bounced on her toes. "I hope he finds his lost city of metal someday. I hope you all do." It looked like she wanted to leave with us in search of it right now.

"We're about to sit on a cart full of rocks and hang out in the wind," Brock said. "Wanna come?"

Alondra laughed. "As much as I want to, I think I'd better stay here." She reached for Ruben's reins, and the man who rode the cart down took Buck's. "I'll miss you all," Alondra said; then they both headed back toward the path.

Before long, the cart was out in the open, with the two horses hitched to it, the sail lying on top of the seforium like a giant cover.

It took an hour and a half of walking to reach the rickety bridge that crossed over White Rock River and into Desolation Alley. Once we got to the other side, I was more than ready to turn toward home. As we lifted the sail, the sun rose in the distance and made the seforium shine the most beautiful orange I'd ever seen.

"Here we go," Luke said as he placed the sail mast in the hole in the middle of the cart. Then he led us out into the wind.

Aaren and I rode on the cart first, and practiced a bit to figure out how to steer. As soon as we got the hang of it, I realized that we were only going at the speed of walking.

"Luke?" I called out. "Is this as fast as we'll go?"

He chuckled. "No. The wind isn't as strong the closer to the river you get. I figured you'd want a chance to get used to it before we threw you into Desolation Alley. Are you ready?"

I'd been ready since I first heard their idea of using a cart and sail.

"Go about fifty feet that direction, and you'll be in the thick of it. We'll keep the horses near the river and out of the wind—try to go the same speed as us."

We veered to the left. The wind caught the sail and jerked us ahead, then made us fly forward. The trees on my right whipped by faster than I've ever seen them pass me. It took every bit of our focus to steer over all the bumps and rocks in the dirt. We were probably going twice as fast as the fastest I've ever raced a horse before.

The horses!

I had been paying so much attention to the path, I'd forgotten that we were supposed to go their speed. I twisted in the seat. The horses were so far behind us, they looked like little bugs. I tugged on Aaren's sleeve and yelled, "Slow down!" I pointed to the right, so he'd get what I meant even if he couldn't hear me over the wind. He did, and we adjusted the wheels, slowing as we got farther and farther from the center of Desolation Alley. Eventually, we reached the side of the river, where the wind barely moved us, and then waited for Luke and Brock.

It was too bad we couldn't go as fast as the wind would take us. We'd make it home to White Rock in no time! But we'd need the horses for the last 125 miles, and if they were days behind us, it really wouldn't matter that we got there more quickly.

When Brock and Luke caught up, I jumped off the seat to give Brock a turn. "You're going to love this," I said.

Brock and Aaren stayed closer to the speed of the horses than Aaren and I had. We took turns trading off about every hour. Sometimes I was with Brock, sometimes with Aaren, and sometimes with Luke.

I couldn't believe that Luke and his dad had come this entire distance, but traveling the other direction, the wind in their faces the whole time. It never stopped blowing!

At the end of the day, we set up camp in the middle of some poor wind-beaten trees as close to the river and away from the worst of the wind as we could get. We detached the sail, set it down on the ground, untied our bedding from the frame, and laid our bedrolls on top of the frame so it wouldn't blow away. Then we sat on the bedrolls while we ate so they wouldn't be lost to the wind, either. Before crawling into bed, the three of us told Luke about Anna's theories and what we figured out. When I explained that ruthenium could hold a permanent magnetic charge, his eyes went from surprised to excited to eager.

"You're going to find the ruthenium, aren't you?"

He gave me that mischievous smile that made him

look like a kid who was planning something fun. I hoped he would find it.

"How far do you think we traveled today?" Aaren asked.

Luke looked back at the road. "Let's just say 'far.'"


By the fourth day of our trip back, I was sore from sitting on the hard bench of the bumpy cart or on the hard saddle of the bumpy horse, but the fun of flying across the ground in the cart never got old. I wondered if this was what riding in a car felt like before the bombs.

When we stopped for lunch, we saw Glacier in the distance across the river. That meant we were nearly 125 miles from home! We hadn't seen another person on our side of the river the whole time.

My skin was so dry from the constant wind, it was cracking. I tried to get my fingers through my hair to pull it into a ponytail, and Aaren laughed at me. "When we get back, it's going to take weeks to brush through that mess."

Aaren had needed a haircut before we left, and it had gotten even longer since we'd been gone. "We're going have to shave you bald!" I said.

"While mine," Brock said as he tried to flip his hair out of his eyes, except it was so tangled, it moved as one solid mass, "has stayed perfect."

* * *

In the middle of day five, the cart was going slower than the horses no matter where we aimed it.

Luke rode over. "We've reached the end of Desolation Alley."

I looked behind me at the land we'd crossed, where it fell off into the sky so far away. My lips, skin, and hair were glad to see Desolation Alley gone. The part of me that loves to sky jump was heartbroken. I didn't know if I'd ever be able to travel that far again, or spend nearly five days sailing across the land in a cart.

I thought back to the thrill of figuring out what Anna had been trying to solve all along. Something about exploring and discovering things felt more like me than inventing ever had. But even though I was going to miss this, I didn't want to be the same as Luke and always be out here. In front of me, White Rock was finally visible. It was teeny on the horizon, but it called me home. Not everything about me came from my birth family—I got a lot of things from my parents and even from my town. That part of me wanted to be back. To see my family.

To be home.

# Home

Early the next afternoon, with the horses pulling the cart, we circled around the back side of our crater enough to see Browning. It wasn't home, but it was a familiar sight, and it meant the tunnel to White Rock was only ten miles farther.

Then I heard a sound, like a far-off roar. I whipped my head to it—back toward Browning. The main gates were open, and people were streaming out. All of them were shouting. It took a minute before I realized that the shouts we were hearing were actually cheers.

"Why are the people of Browning out here?" I asked.

"I don't think those are the people of Browning," Brock said.

I squinted when the ones on horses got close enough that we could start to see faces. The riders were from White Rock! But the only faces I really saw were the two on the front horse—my parents. My dad rode right up to us, grabbed his injured leg, and slid down, then held out a hand to help my mom.

"You're safe! You're back!" my mom repeated as she checked to make sure all my body parts were still attached.

More and more people reached us, all talking at the same time.

"What's going on?" I asked.

"The rest of the group made it back late last night," my dad said. "Without you." His voice cracked on the last two words. I looked from him to my mom and noticed their red swollen eyes.

My mom motioned to two trailers outside of Browning's gate. "A rescue party was just leaving to go save you."

My dad glanced at the cart of seforium. "I should've known that it'd be you saving us."

"Did we get here in time?" Brock asked Mr. Hudson.

Mr. Hudson smiled. "You did."

We did it. We actually did it.

I turned to my parents. "Why were you in Browning?"

My dad took a deep breath before answering. "We were watching the horizon. As a town, we agreed that if we didn't see any sign of you by three days ago, we'd evacuate."

"What?" I said. "The entire town is in Browning?"

"Every last one of us," my dad said. "They've been good to have us."

Brenna came running up to us, ahead of the rest of Aaren's family, and wrapped her arms around Aaren's legs. "I missed you!" Then she reached out an arm to me, squishing the three of us together. "What did you bring me?"

"What? I—" Aaren fumbled.

"You didn't let me go with you, and then you forgot about me?"

I rifled through my bag. "Of course we didn't forget you." I pulled out the piece of pavement I had found when I went to Downwind. It had almost completely slipped my mind. I hadn't even shown it to Aaren or Brock. I put it in her hand and said, "We brought this back for you. It's what the roads were made out of before the bombs."

Brenna looked up at us as if she'd never seen anything so amazing. "Really? This is for me?"

I nodded, and she brushed her fingers across it a few times. After a moment, she said, "I was faking asleep when Mr. Williams came last night to tell Mom and Dad what happened. Mom freaked out."

Aaren sighed. "She's never letting me go anywhere again."

I heard my name called. I turned to see Luke, standing as though he wasn't going to walk any farther.

"Luke?" I said. "Are you—" But then I didn't need to ask. I saw it in his eyes. "You're not staying."

He shook his head.

I tried not to be sad. I didn't think he would stay anyway—he had a lost city of metal to find. "Will I see you again?"

"You will. I know you're glad to be back home, but someday I'll stop by to ask if you're up to leaving again to make a world-changing discovery."

"Do you promise?"

"I promise. We'll race horses at an inappropriate time again soon."

I reached out and shook his hand. "Deal."

We stood next to the cracks in the earth, where Mr. Hudson and his team had crushed the seforium into powder, readying it to be spread in the crevices. Instead of looking in the cracks, though, I couldn't pull my eyes away from the Bomb's Breath. The gray that had looked like haze before was now so thick that I couldn't see the sky above it. White Rock was thrown into shadows enough that it felt like dusk. And it was so low! I knew that it was dropping at a continually faster pace and that it would be almost to the top of the tunnel—less than five feet above my head—by the time we got back. I just didn't anticipate how suffocated it would make me feel.

"No wonder they evacuated," Brock said.

I spotted a tree with an oddly shaped trunk that had the bottom of one branch below the Bomb's Breath. The rest of it disappeared into the gray. As I kept my eye on it, I swore I could see the grayness lowering.

"Do you three want to throw in the first of it?" Mr. Hudson said.

I put my hands together and scooped up as much of the orange powder as I could hold; then Brock and Aaren walked with me to the edge of the crevice.

The three of us tossed our handfuls into the opening. The orange powder blew into a cloud as it fell to the bottom. Mr. Hudson's team started shoveling the seforium along the entire length of the crevices, and we grabbed shovels and helped.

Once all of it was spread along the openings, my dad stood next to me and we both stared up at the Bomb's Breath.

"I think it's working!" Aaren called out.

I squinted up to the grayness in the Bomb's Breath.

Was it getting lighter? It was so hard to tell. I found the tree I had been watching and kept staring at that bottom branch. "It is!" I yelled. "I can see it moving up!"

I was so happy, I wanted to shout that we did it to everyone *everywhere*. We all stood in silence, our heads toward the skies, watching as everything changed so slowly, we hardly noticed it was changing at all. Until we saw the blue sky again, peeking through the gray more and more.

My dad looked over at me. "You seem different now," he said.

"It's my new hairdo." I smoothed my windblown hair, which I was pretty sure I'd never get a comb through again.

My dad touched my hair, as if it was some fascinating science experiment that Mr. Hudson had made. "Nope. That's not it. I think it's that you . . . look older."

"Really?" I said.

He examined me closely, trying to guess what the change was. I wondered if he'd see that I figured out a lot of things about not giving up. And that I wasn't just like my parents or just like my birth family—that I was somewhere in the middle. Or that I realized I might be good at discovering things, and that we made a discovery that might someday change the world.

Or maybe he couldn't see past the windblown hair. I couldn't blame him.

# Acknowledgments

In many ways, writing book two in a series is more difficult than writing book one, and I relied on my core group of support so much more. A few people deserve greater thanks than I could ever do justice on a couple of pages.

Many thanks and much gratitude go to my family, especially to my husband, Lance, for all his help with brainstorming plotting, giving feedback, providing encouragement, generating ideas, showing unconditional love, covering for me each time writing took me away from home, and making me laugh (especially when I have "Tuesday Face"). I love you, sweetie! To my kids, Kyle, Cory, and Alecia—thanks for all the encouragement, the prayers, the laughs, the support, and the love. You are even more amazing than you know (and you already know you're pretty amazing). To my siblings, for making sure my life growing up was full of adventure (and only occasionally full of peril); my parents, for believing we were capable of doing big things on our own (and for going on dates every Friday night, leaving us to some creative boredom busting); and my sister Kristine for being the kind of adult that made me want her as a best friend (and a trusted assistant).

To my editor, Shana Corey, who is brilliant and insightful and kind and dedicated and isn't afraid to suggest big changes that'll make the book infinitely better—thank you times a million! (My book thanks you, too. It knows how much better it is under your direction.)

To my agent, Sara Crowe—thanks for being encouraging when I need encouragement, for being excited when I'm excited, for being calm when I'm stressed, and for being amazing all the time.

I'm grateful that Sky Jumpers found a home at Random House. I owe many people thanks for helping it get into the hands of so many readers. Especially Nicole Banholzer, my remarkable publicist, who is incredible and a joy to work with; Paula Sadler, who is delightful (and has the most beautiful handwriting!); Mallory Loehr, my phenomenal publisher; Nicole de las Heras, for her art direction; Alison Kolani, who is a fantastic copy chief; Adrienne Waintraub, for getting my book into school libraries and promoting it at conferences; and sales, for all their tireless work.

Many thanks to my critique partners. To Erin Summerill, who is not only an impressive sounding board, but spunky, energetic, stylish, serious, lighthearted, and loyal, all wrapped into one. To Jessie Humphries, who is loving, happy, helpful, fun, and supportive (and doesn't let a little thing like a six-hour drive stop her from being here anytime she's needed). To Rob Code, the setting and arc master, and Jason Manwaring, emotion and logic savant. To Elana Johnson. Dude. I owe you so much more than cookies. If I listed all the ways you've helped over the years, it would take pages. Hulk smash! And Clint Johnson—you definitely should've been thanked in book one for being an insightful critiquer and helping a new author find her way. To Skipper Coates, scientist extraordinaire: your brain is incredible. I brought an armful of random geology-shaped puzzle pieces, and you helped me make a picture.

I'm privileged to be a part of some fantastic writing groups. A huge thank-you to the Lucky 13s, the League of Extraordinary Writers, Eight Times Up, all of the Storymakers, the Rock Canyon group, and the Writing Group of Joy and Awesomeness—you girls definitely live up to your name. Chantele Sedgwick, Katie Dodge, Ruth Josse, Kim Krey, Donna Nolan, Jeigh Meredith, Taffy Lovell,

Julie Donaldson, Sandy Ponton, Julie Maughon, Shelly Morris, Christene Houston, and Jamie Thompson—let's laugh long into the night again soon.

Most of all, much gratitude to everyone who reads *The Forbidden Flats*. Your kind words and the way you've enthusiastically shared *Sky Jumpers* with your friends has meant the world to me. Thank you.

# About the Author

PEGGY EDDLEMAN lives at the foot of the Rocky Mountains in Utah with her husband and their three kids. In addition to writing, Peggy has worked as a newspaper delivery girl, a software tester, a fast-food worker, a bank teller, a technical writer, and a tutor for fourth graders. You can visit Peggy online at peggyeddleman.com or on Twitter at @PeggyEddleman.